D1547569

DEATH COMES TO SANTA FE

Also by Amanda Allen

Santa Fe Revival mysteries

SANTA FE MOURNING
A MOMENT IN CRIME

DEATH COMES TO SANTA FE

Amanda Allen

SEVERN
HOUSE

First world edition published in Great Britain and the USA in 2023
by Severn House, an imprint of Canongate Books Ltd,
14 High Street, Edinburgh EH1 1TE.

severnhouse.com

Copyright © Amanda Allen, 2023

All rights reserved including the right of
reproduction in whole or in part in any form.
The right of Amanda Allen to be identified
as the author of this work has been asserted
in accordance with the Copyright,
Designs & Patents Act 1988.

British Library Cataloguing-in-Publication Data
A CIP catalogue record for this title is available from the British Library.

ISBN-13: 978-1-4483-1099-9 (cased)
ISBN-13: 978-1-4483-1100-2 (e-book)

This is a work of fiction. Names, characters, places and incidents
are either the product of the author's imagination or are used fictitiously.
Except where actual historical events and characters are being described
for the storyline of this novel, all situations in this publication are
fictitious and any resemblance to actual persons, living or dead,
business establishments, events or locales is purely coincidental.

All Severn House titles are printed on acid-free paper.

Typeset by Palimpsest Book Production Ltd.,
Falkirk, Stirlingshire, Scotland.
Printed and bound in Great Britain by
TJ Books, Padstow, Cornwall.

Praise for Amanda Allen

"A satisfying read for Maddie fans; it's also a good bet to give fans of Jessica Fellowes' The Mitford Murders (2018)."
Booklist on *A Moment in Crime*

"Readers will appreciate Allen's likable group of characters, acute attention to historical details, and cameos of such real-life celebrities as poet Alice Henderson and her artist husband, William Henderson. Fans will be eager for Maddie's next adventure."
Publishers Weekly on *A Moment in Crime*

"Auspicious . . . Readers will want to see more of the appealing Maddie, whose next adventure is hinted at in the epilogue."
Publishers Weekly on *Santa Fe Mourning*

"Allen's re-creation of 1920s language, dress, and clashing norms helps create an immersive whodunit, and Maddie is sure to become a beloved heroine."
Booklist on *Santa Fe Mourning*

"Spoiled NY Flapper meets the Wild West – what could be more delightful?"
– Rhys Bowen, New York Times bestselling author

"Engrossing . . . With evocative descriptions and captivating historical detail, Amanda Allen paints a vivid picture of post-WWI Santa Fe and weaves a mystery that is sure to keep you guessing until the end!"
– Ashley Weaver, author of the Edgar Finalist Murder at the Brightwell on *Santa Fe Mourning*

"For fans of Miss Fisher's Murder mysteries . . . A mystery with the tang of bootleg hooch and the sharp bite of poison."
– Kate Parker, author of the Deadly Series and the Victorian Bookshop mysteries

About the author

Amanda Allen wrote her first book at the age of sixteen – a vast historical epic starring all her friends as the characters, written secretly during algebra class.

She's never since used algebra, but her books have been nominated for many awards, including the RITA Award, the Romantic Times Reviewers' Choice Award, the Booksellers Best, the National Readers Choice Award, and the Holt Medallion. She lives in Santa Fe with two rescue dogs, a wonderful husband, and far too many books and royal memorabilia collections.

PROLOGUE
Santa Fe, September 1924

'Burn him! Burn him!' The shout went up into the purple-black night sky, eager, full of laughter, touched with just a bit of anxiety. Madeline Vaughn-Alwin glanced around at the faces of her friends, barely lit with the few torches planted around the garden, and shivered.

Will Shuster, her artist friend, had outdone himself with this project. Everyone was still shouting, dancing, when a burst of fireworks exploded over their heads, a sparkling bouquet of red, green, blue, gold. The light shimmered on Will's giant puppet up on his dais, ghostly white in his long paper skirt, except for a shock of bright green hair. His enormous eyes, painted black and ringed in red, stared down at them wrathfully, his immense bat ears flapping in the breeze.

They'd spent a week building him out of wire, wood, wool, and cotton, painting him, stuffing him with everyone's written woes. Zozobra – gloom. Now they would execute him, and destroy their problems to move free into the future.

As a bell tolled, Maddie reached for David's hand and held on to it tightly. He gave it a reassuring squeeze, making her smile.

Zozobra's long arms fluttered upward, his red-painted slash of a mouth opening and closing, emitting a rough growl. A group of Maddie's artist friends, who also fancied themselves musicians, started pounding their drums and blasting their trumpets from the shadows. It was all very enthusiastic, but very out of tune, and combined with Zozo's growling it was deafening. Maddie laughed, and let go of David to clap her hands over her ears.

'Burn him!' the cry went up again. '*Que viva la fiesta!*'

She looked forward to this week every year since she moved to Santa Fe, the time when the city celebrated the moment three hundred years ago when Don Diego de Vargas marched back into Santa Fe after being driven out twelve years before in the great Pueblo Revolt. It was a few days of pageantry, as the man given the honor of portraying Don Diego and the young lady voted La Reina and her princessly court led the city's old families in special Masses at the cathedral, processions, dances. And, since Will and the others had come to town, silly touches as well, like parades and masked balls.

And burning the glooms of the year.

Maddie studied Zozobra as he moaned and flailed, and wondered what the real Don Diego would have thought about all this as he sat in his camp outside Santa Fe centuries ago. As he prayed to La Conquistadora, the wooden Holy Mary statue who fled Santa Fe with the Spanish and returned with them, and now resided in a gilded chapel at the cathedral to be paraded around every year in September. He had prayed to her, it was said, to help him reenter the city without shedding blood. If she let him do so, he told her, he would throw her a party every year.

And so they did, every autumn at Fiesta. But hundreds of years of Masses and family parties were turning into ghostly burnings, dancing, drinking.

Will climbed up on to the dais, his rumpled red hair glowing in the torchlight, his paint-stained hands waving much like Zozo's. The light reflected in his round spectacles. 'My friends! Thank you for being here tonight, and for all your hard work in gathering our glooms. Here's to their destruction, and a bright new year ahead of us! *Que viva la fiesta!*'

The poet Witter Bynner, Santa Fe's master of ceremonies if there was one, paraded past in a long black cloak, a torch held high, followed by a procession of red-clad glooms moaning and singing.

Everyone cheered and whistled as he tossed a flaming torch at Zozobra's feet, and flames touched and licked at the papiermâché. It caught and spread, crackling higher and higher, the smoke curling around the vast, tangled garden and into the night sky. As his bulbous head burst into flame, his face melted, his eyes backlit and demonic. Sparks flew up toward the stars, and his arms flailed faster, caught helplessly in the glooms he had created.

One big, cleansing moment.

More flames shot up, popping loudly. Maddie laughed, and closed her eyes, holding tight to David. She hadn't many glooms, it was true; her painting was going better than ever, her studio behind her Canyon Road house filling with work for a new exhibition, her feelings for the handsome English doctor growing and growing. Her little created family in that house were happy, too, with Juanita's twins at the Loretto School, Eddie being promoted at his job at La Fonda Hotel, Juanita baking up a delicious storm every day, when she wasn't writing to her handsome movie actor suitor in Los Angeles. It had been a good year, a happy one. Yet somehow the fire, the moaning demon, created a touch of cold disquiet somewhere deep inside of her. She wrapped her arms around David and held him close.

'Dance with me!' she cried as the music swung into a wild waltz. He laughed, and twirled her around and around in the dying flames, the expanding night, the stars that seemed to sparkle just within her reach as they only did in New Mexico.

Maddie blinked open her eyes as the rose-gold light of morning pierced her sleep. She groaned and rolled over, finding not her own fluffy bed with its bright quilts and soft sheets but the thin cushions of the old iron chaise on Will's portal. She laughed to realize she must have fallen asleep there after dancing for hours, and rubbed at her mussed, bobbed hair.

The day smelled of the freshness of morning, the flowers growing wild in the garden, the tinge of smoke from Zozobra's death throes. She stretched and sat up as she studied the people around her, slumped on pillows on the portal, sleeping in hammocks. Will was poking through the ashes, a frown creasing his lean face behind his spectacles.

'Will?' she called, finding her shoes before she stepped down off the portal. 'Is something wrong?'

He glanced up, his eyes wide. He gestured to the metal backbone of Zozobra, the pitted dais, which was all that remained of the demon. 'I think Zozo got more than he bargained for last night, Maddie.'

He poked his rake at the smoking ashes again. The slips of paper they all wrote their glooms on were gone, but something else gleamed there, smoke-stained but intact. Something she hadn't seen when they sewed Zozo closed the day before.

A set of false teeth, pale ivory still attached to fake gums. A pocket watch, the silver marred by the dark gray ashes. The mangled gold frames of a pair of spectacles.

Maddie swallowed hard. 'Those weren't there before.'

'No. Neither was this.' Will used a small spade to hold up something else. A human finger bone and the remains of a burned shoe.

'Nertz,' Maddie cursed. It looked like her idyllic year was ending.

ONE

A Few Weeks Earlier

'Oh, Señora Maddie! That was the saddest thing I have ever seen.' Juanita Anaya, Maddie's housekeeper and dearest friend, took an embroidered handkerchief from her handbag and dabbed at her eyes as they stepped from the dim lobby of the El Onate movie house into the bright autumn light. Everyone else around them was sniffling, too.

Maddie blinked at Juanita in astonishment. Juanita was not usually given to shows of emotion – it was always hard to tell what she was really thinking or feeling, everything she did was to comfort (or usually feed) someone else. But Maddie had to agree with her; *The Far Sunset* was indeed sad, and filled with romance and thrills and the beauty of the mountains where it was filmed. 'I can't believe we actually saw them film those scenes, right here, practically in our own back garden! I was sure we were right there a hundred years ago, on that ranch.'

She also couldn't believe now there had been a murder behind the scenes of those grand vistas. Life had been so filled with lovelier things since then, with art and friends and – dare she think it? – romance. Real romance, not movie swooning.

Juanita tucked away her handkerchief and took Maddie's arm as they set off across the plaza. It was filled with people hurrying around putting up the decorations for Fiesta, the bunting and streamers on the bandstand, the wooden family crests that would hang from the portal of the Palace of the Governors, the food booths being hammered together. 'That Mrs Luther, she certainly proved to be a talented director!'

Maddie nodded, thinking about what a terrible time Bridget Luther had with her husband the famous director – until he was murdered, and she took over the movie as director. It was the second murder Maddie had found herself solving, after Juanita's husband was killed. 'Mrs Godwin now, remember? Remember those pics last month in *Silver Screen*?' She sighed to remember those gorgeous images of acres of satin and gardenias, of Bridget Luther's glowing face under Brussels lace as she beamed at her dishy new millionaire husband. Not that Maddie could be entirely convinced by those beaming photos; Bridget Luther had been a hard-headed businesswoman if ever there was one. But it was still difficult not get pitter-pattered at such beauty.

And maybe, just maybe, deep down in her secret heart, all that lace and orange blossoms made her think a bit about a certain English doctor with sky-blue eyes and luscious kisses . . .

Maddie almost giggled like a schoolgirl to remember the first time she saw David on that train coming home to Santa Fe. Those gorgeous eyes, his sunlit smile. And all the days since, holding hands, talking about anything and everything. And his kisses. Yum!

Juanita seemed to sense some of Maddie's daydreams, because she squeezed her arm and gave a little smile. 'Mrs Luther's, er, Mrs Godwin's, gown was so pretty, *sí*? I'm sure I could copy those sleeves in no time for you.'

Maddie laughed, and squeezed back. 'Then you should copy them for yourself, Juanita. Wasn't it larky to see Mr Altumara there on the screen? He was quite the bee's knees.'

Juanita, a widowed mother of three who was usually the essence of elegant dignity, actually blushed. Rosy spots flooded across her high cheekbones, making Maddie giggle. Francisco, Frank, Altumara was a girlhood flame of Juanita's from the pueblo who had gone off to be an actor and resurfaced at the ill-fated *Far Sunset* set. He was a real looker, that was true, and had seemed as taken with Juanita as ever.

'It's a fine thing he can't hear you, Señora Maddie,' Juanita said as they crossed the dusty lane of Canyon Road toward home. 'He was always too full of himself when we were children! I admit, he hasn't done so badly, though.'

'I should say not! We've seen him in three movies already besides this one. Have you heard from him lately?'

'He wrote in July, on set in Arizona somewhere. He says he might be home at the pueblo for Christmas.'

'Then you must go, too. I'm sure Eddie and the twins would love it.' Eddie, Juanita's son, was almost grown now, working at La Fonda as a waiter and busboy, learning all he could about running a hotel so he could move up the ranks one day. The girls were still at the Loretto School, but they, too, were growing faster than Maddie could believe.

Juanita sighed. 'Eduardo would say he is too busy at that job of his! I'm glad he's doing so well there, I was so worried about him when his father died. But he has much to learn from my brothers, too. He needs to remember where we come from.'

Maddie nodded. She always wanted to *forget* where she came from, that stultifying mansion on Fifth Avenue where she could never be herself, never make her own choices. It was only once she was widowed, once she set off on a cross-country train journey and found herself staying in Santa Fe, that she could make her own life. But it was so different for Juanita and her children. Juanita came from the pueblo at San Ildefonso where her family had lived for centuries. They belonged somewhere, and Maddie rather envied that. 'I'm sure Anton at La Fonda would be happy to give him days off. He says Eddie is his very best worker, he won't ever want to lose him!'

Juanita smiled proudly. 'Well, right now Eddie is too busy getting ready for Fiesta, as the whole town is. La Fonda is completely full! Everyone has work to do now. As do you, Señora Maddie.'

'I am! Not that I'm complaining. I do love this time of year.' Santa Fe held their Fiesta every September, created to mark the return of Don Diego de Vargas to New Mexico in 1692. There had been processions and special Masses since 1712, but only recently, since statehood in 1912, had parades and dances and all-around fun been added. It grew every year, until now, in protest at the commercialization by Eastern companies that had started charging fees to actually enter Fiesta events, Maddie's artist friends had added parades and costumes. The Pasatiempo, they called it.

'The dances and music and parties. The food! Especially your green chile stew,' Maddie said.

'My recipe is not so bad,' Juanita said modestly. She was well known all around town as one of the best cooks there was; Alice Henderson and the wealthy White sisters were constantly trying to lure her from Maddie. But Juanita would never admit it herself; she was not one to boast. 'That friend of yours, Señor Shuster, though – he will work you to a thread for all his party schemes! I've never known someone with so much energy. He is one *loco* Anglo! It must come from that red hair.'

Maddie laughed. Will Shuster *did* have vivid hair, wild as a burning haystack, and the spirit to match. His Pasatiempo included parades, for children and pets and adults alike, chances to dress in costumes, dance, sing. And to kick it all off, Zozobra, old man gloom, would go up in flames.

'I'm having a lot of fun building Zozo,' Maddie said. She glanced at the slim platinum watch on her wrist, and cried, 'Oh! I'm nearly late for Señora Montoya's portrait sitting.'

'We should hurry, then,' Juanita said firmly, and matched her steps to her words. 'The Montoyas are such a fine family in town! They can get you so many commissions, Señora Maddie.'

They turned at the familiar dusty intersection of Canyon Road, where dogs slept in the shade of an ancient horse-chestnut tree and chickens clucked around the dirt lane. They passed the old brick schoolhouse with its gleaming white Victorian cupola, now an art studio, the little grocery store where old men napped under the portal, the adobe houses with their opened doors and bright flowers in their window boxes, goats tethered to fence posts. All so unlike the crowded New York streets where she grew up. But even there people prepared for Fiesta, hanging streamers along their portal posts.

Her own house, the precious little place she bought with her own money from Peter, her late husband, and her grandmother's trust and thus untouchable by her family, waited just past the turn to Garcia Street. A tall adobe wall fronted Canyon Road, hiding her own shady portal – what her parents called a veranda at their Newport 'cottage' – and the large garden behind a gate painted bright blue. The blue shutters on the narrow windows were closed against the afternoon sun.

They stepped into the front courtyard, flagstone floor dotted with blue and purple pots overflowing with red, yellow, and white flowers, vivid against the tan stucco walls. The main door was propped open to let the autumn breeze in.

Maddie had adored the old house, almost as old as the 1712 Fiesta, the first time she set eyes on it, with its whitewashed interior walls, its long, narrow sitting room with dark viga ceilings and a fireplace at each end faced with blue tiles that kept the chilly nights at bay. It had been built on for two hundred years as the families grew and was like a wonderful maze.

Narrow corridors radiated out from the sitting room to bedrooms, small studies, and the dining room, with the kitchen at the back. The furniture was sparse, unlike her parents' houses stuffed with satin chairs, marble tables, vases, and knickknacks. Hand-painted chairs and sofas from Spain, scattered with embroidered cushions, shelves overflowing with books, brilliantly colored artwork on the walls made it cozy and cheerful. Gray and red Navajo rugs were scattered on the polished floor, along with the twins' dolls and toys from their terrier Buttercup and new poodle Pansy. The only new piece was a piano for the twins' music lessons. It was her own timeless refuge – with new plumbing and electricity, of course.

'Don't keep Señora Montoya waiting,' Juanita reminded her.

'If she likes her portrait, then we can enlarge the kitchen!' Maddie laughed, but she knew Juanita was right. Ricardo Montoya was from a very old Santa Fe family, and had built up one of the largest business concerns in the whole town. And Catalina Montoya, who was once a Gomez and also from an old family, was so easy to work with, beautiful and kind, ready with a soft laugh and full of information about the Fiesta parties and all her Santa Fe friends and their family histories. Maddie's art career had been growing; she'd been selling more pieces, local landscapes to tourists, portraits. But she needed to grow even more. 'If only all my sitters were like her . . .'

Juanita took off her good blue wool coat and flower-trimmed

hat as she made her way toward the kitchen, and Maddie grabbed an apple from the painted side table before she hurried toward the studio at the back of her garden. The dogs Buttercup and Pansy, sensing something interesting in the offing, crawled out of their cushy monogrammed beds to pad after her.

Gunther Ryder, her neighbor and good friend, was hard at work at his typewriter under the shade of his portal just next door, his dark red hair gleaming. He waved, and called, 'Dinner at La Fonda tonight, darling? I have a new cravat, heavenly shade of rose madder with polka dots! So *au courant*.'

'We can't let a good cravat go to waste!' she called back. Gunther was utterly addicted to cravats, only one of his many endearing qualities. 'You can be my escort. David has to work late at the hospital, he'll meet us there when they finally let him go.'

'Oh, the dishy doctor! Right-ho. I'll bring over a pitcher of my Pink Ladies before, you can tell me how your latest masterpiece progresses.' He was as good at mixing up cocktails, sourced from mysterious connections, as he was at writing best-selling novels.

She hurried through her garden, like the house a carefully created haven of beauty, with towering old horse-chestnut trees and one ancient salt cedar the twins liked to climb, laid out with winding gravel paths and flower beds. In the summer it would burst into color and scent, with honeysuckle climbing the walls, white and yellow and pink roses, lavender and rosemary. Even now, in autumn, it was filled with colors, scarlet and amber and chamisa-yellow. A swing hung from one tree, and two dog houses sat in the corners. To one side was Juanita's casita, and to the other the studio, once a tool shed she had carefully renovated.

It had a skylight now, and lots of windows, with shelves for supplies and sliding cabinets for finished canvases. Her easel was at the far end, with a table for palettes and paint boxes, and there was a raised dais draped in faded red velvet for models. Photos and postcards were tucked on corkboards for inspiration. The air was warm and dusty, heavy with the scents of oil paints and linseed.

The most delicious perfume in the world, she thought.

She threw back all the window shutters, letting in a flood of light. This was the one place Juanita never cleaned, so the shelves were dusty and the old blue rug on the floor needed a beating. A few half-finished paintings were propped along the walls, and sketchbooks were piled everywhere.

Maddie stepped into the shadows of the deeper studio, the dogs trotting in behind her to flop down on the faded rug and watch her.

She unpinned her new Reboux silk and straw cloche hat, a gift from her stylish cousin Gwen in California, and shrugged on a paint-stained smock, then she carefully studied her latest 'masterpiece'. Not quite ready for the Louvre, or even the Fine Arts Museum a few miles away on Palace Street, maybe, but not so very bad. Catalina looked elegant, as usual, the folds of her green taffeta gown shimmering, but something, some essence, was missing . . .

Maddie had just arranged the dais with a brown brocade chair brought from the Montoya house and an embroidered shawl to drape across it, and mixed up some colors on her palette when a soft knock sounded on the door.

'Mrs Alwin?' Catalina Montoya said, peeking inside. She was not a tall woman, but slim and with perfect posture, with shining dark hair barely touched with gray and large green eyes, and an oval face with high cheekbones and a Grecian nose. A perfect model, really, if not for the shadows that sometimes lurked within her eyes. 'Are you ready for me? I'm afraid I'm rather early.'

'Oh, yes, very nearly, Mrs Montoya! Do come in.' The dogs leaped up enthusiastically to greet her, Maddie scolding them that they would ruin her fine amber-colored wool and satin paneled skirt, but Catalina just laughed and petted them, cooing. 'You two, do stop being such pests! I am a terrible dog trainer, I'm afraid.'

Catalina laughed. 'I don't mind, they are so very sweet. I had terriers just like them when I was a little *niña*, I do wish I could have one now. Little dogs are such friends. But my husband does not like them.' For an instant, her lovely oval face under the brim of her velvet hat seemed a bit sad, but she quickly shook it off to smile.

She glanced around the studio, noticing the two panes of painted glass propped against one wall. The red flowers in blue vases, with touches of yellow daisies, gleamed with springtime. 'You are doing these for the portal at La Fonda, yes?'

'Oh, yes,' Maddie said enthusiastically, as she tried to get just the right amount of white into a bit of rose paint. 'They're replacing some of the skylights, and asked me to contribute some. I was very excited!' The main courtyard at La Fonda, open to the sky, along with the North Portal that was covered and lit with skylights, had once been plain glass, but Olive Rush, the force of nature that ran the Museum of Fine Arts, had decided to commission local artists to paint the glass instead.

'Then I will be able to point to them and tell everyone my own portrait was done by that same famous artist!' Catalina said. She sat down on her chair and arranged herself in her usual pose, her hands folded in the lap of her Chanel suit, head slightly tilted down.

'May your words be a prophecy!' Maddie laughed. 'I'm hoping at least one will be installed before the Fiesta parties.'

'Yes, my husband is hosting a dinner there one night. Our daughter Sofia is one of the Queen's court. Perhaps next year she will be La Reina herself. That is what Ricardo hopes.' A frown drifted over Catalina's pink-painted lips. To be voted as La Reina, the queen of the Fiesta, leading her royal court, was a great honor, vied for by the young daughters of all the local families.

'And is that what Sofia hopes, too?' Maddie asked, mixing a bit more paint on her palette.

'Of course. Families come from all over the state for the Fiesta celebrations, families with fine sons. She can meet so many young men! More than when she was at the Loretto School, of course, though the sisters gave her the finest education.'

The twins were at the Loretto School, too, and Maddie knew it was a good education. Languages, mathematics, science, as well as embroidery and dancing. But the sisters were very strict indeed. 'I am sure it wasn't quite a hot-bed of romance!

Yet surely Sofia has plenty of beaux. She's so beautiful.' And so she was, just like her mother.

Catalina smiled, that smile fading at the mention of her daughter. 'She is. She looks just like my own mother did! And she does indeed have suitors. No one has her father's approval yet, though.'

'And your son? Is he in Don Diego's court?' The man voted Don Diego every year also led a court of knights, who accompanied him on processions and in the Grand Entrada to the plaza at the start of Fiesta.

'Juan-Antonio? No. Not this year. He is – well, so very busy.' Catalina glanced away, staring out the window at the garden. Usually subjects were rather chatty while being painted, but Catalina was often reserved, careful, her gossip of the most benign sort. A bit like Juanita in some ways. Every word measured until they trusted you.

Maddie, too, worked quietly for a while, until she smiled and said, 'And how are the plans for your dinner? The one for Sofia.'

As Maddie tried to capture just the right glints of auburn in Catalina's lustrous dark hair, they chatted lightly about Fiesta dos, including the Montoyas' planned dinner and a masked 'Ferdinand and Isabella' ball at La Fonda, and Catalina seemed to cheer up a bit.

Just as the sun from the windows started to shift, turning faintly golden at the edges, there was a quick knock at the studio door, making the dogs lift their heads and Catalina's shoulders tense again.

'Señora Maddie?' Juanita called. 'Señor Montoya's car is waiting for Señora Montoya.'

Catalina's expression flickered, almost panicked for an instant, and she reached for her hat and gloves, her hand shaking. 'How has time flown so fast? You are a wonderful distraction, Mrs Alwin. I must hurry!' She stepped down from the dais, straightening her skirt, fussing with her beaded handbag. 'You will come to our dinner, yes? Do bring Dr Cole.'

'I would love to, and so would he. Thank you.' Maddie had to admit she was rather dying to see the inside of the Montoya house, said to be one of the largest in town. She handed Catalina her hat, and followed her out to the street.

It wasn't just any car waiting there, but a rare, expensive, gleamingly gorgeous Pierce Arrow with a uniformed chauffeur at the wheel. Ricardo Montoya waited at the passenger door, his suit perfectly tailored, his red brocade tie and pocket square and gray hat like something out of a fashion paper. Gunther would have been jealous.

And he was handsome, too, a good match for his beautiful wife, with salt and pepper hair cropped close and chocolate brown eyes in a chiseled face. He wore spectacles whose gold frames glinted in the sun, and his smile was blindingly white. Almost *too* white and straight.

'The famous Señora Alwin! How lovely to meet you at last, my dear. I do hope your paintbrush does my lovely wife justice,' he said, sounding quite affable but also demanding. *Do her justice – or else!*

'It is a beautiful painting, Ricardo,' Catalina chided as the uniformed chauffeur helped her into the luxurious leather backseat. Like the two Montoyas, he was absurdly good-looking, young and slim and smoldering as Ramon Navarro. 'Much too fine for this old face! Mrs Alwin is quite a genius.'

'A genius, eh? I do hope so, since you wouldn't let me engage Mr Sharp.'

Catalina glanced away out the window, her cheeks pink with – was it embarrassment? Mr Sharp was the most sought-after portrait artist in New Mexico. Was Maddie just second best, then? 'He is not nearly so pleasant as Mrs Alwin. I have invited her to dinner soon, along with that charming Dr Cole.'

For an instant, he looked startled, but he quickly smiled. 'Yes, of course you must come, Mrs Alwin. It will be nothing like you are used to in New York, but we do our best to have a fine time in our humble home.'

'I'm sure it will be absolutely spiffing, Mr Montoya. I look forward to it.' She waved at them as the car slid noiselessly away, several of the neighborhood kids gathered around to gawk.

Maddie's own cozy kitchen was a relief after the strange tension of the Montoyas, the sunny floors gleaming and the white ruffled curtains fluttering at the open window, warm and polished and scented with Juanita's fresh apple tarts and the lavender set in a blue vase on the large pine table.

Juanita handed Maddie a bowl of apples and a paring knife, and Maddie set about peeling them. The tree in her garden had a huge crop that season, and she knew the pantry would soon overflow with apple sauce, apple butter, jars of preserved apples, dried apples.

'How was your sitting with Señora Montoya?' Juanita asked, rolling out a crust. The dogs lingered under the table, hoping for a dropped morsel.

'Quite nice. She's so very pretty, such a pleasure to paint, and very sweet. A true old-school European lady, my mother would say.' Her mother, born an Astor, set a great store by old European manners. 'I hadn't really known her before this portrait, just seen her at a few parties.' Maddie ran in more artistic circles than people like the Montoyas, old Santa Fe families whose families had once held land grants from Spanish kings. It was a small town, but it still had its separate cliques.

'Her husband doesn't usually call for her at the end of her sittings,' Juanita said. 'He just sends the car. And such a car! No one else in town has such a thing.'

'Yes, I hadn't seen him here before today. Good looking, isn't he? He invited me to dinner at his house, and it seems they're having a do for their daughter at Fiesta. She's a *princesa* in La Reina's court.'

'Did he, now? A dinner at their house. That would be useful, Señora Maddie, lots of people there who would want their portrait painted.'

'Now you are thinking like a real businesswoman, Juanita!' Maddie laughed. 'But yes, that would be nice. I could use more places to exhibit.'

They were quiet for a moment, the only sounds the companionable thwack of the rolling pin and snick of the knife, the dogs snuffling under the table.

'I wouldn't have thought Sofia Montoya would really want a big Fiesta to-do,' Juanita said.

Maddie thought of the girl she sometimes saw flitting around town, pale-faced, dark-haired, pretty as her mother but shy as a doe. 'Do you know her?'

'She was at the Loretto School a few years ago, and still comes to see Sister Mary Cecilia, who teaches Pearl and Ruby geography. And I see Señorita Montoya once in a while at the lending library. She likes poetry, I think, and romances by Mrs Larsen. A very polite girl, quiet. Always seems to avoid attention, even though everyone wants to know her father.'

'Interesting. Catalina said Sofia is in the royal court this year, and they're hoping she'll be elected La Reina next year.'

'I would think they'd want to see her married before that. She'd be eighteen now, and the queen isn't allowed to be engaged until her reign is over.'

Maddie thought eighteen sounded like an utter baby, especially for a protected, cosseted girl in a small, old town. But then she married her Pete when they were barely older than that, and she lost him in the muddy trenches of war when they were not much more. Maybe Sofia Montoya *wanted* to be married, away from her parents and their expectations. Just like Maddie herself had been. She did feel for the girl.

'Does she have any serious suitors?' she asked.

Juanita thought for a moment, checking the texture of her dough. 'Not that I know of, though Señor Marulis, who does a lot of business with her father, has been seen escorting her to a dinner or dance or two.'

'Señor Marulis!' Maddie exclaimed. 'He must be – I don't know, sixty at least. Though he certainly does seem to run a lot of businesses.'

'Sixty-three,' Juanita said. She seemed so quiet, so dignified, but she always did seem to know who was who. 'He is very wealthy, they say, and could probably be of much help to Señor Montoya if he decides to go into politics.'

'And does Señor Montoya want to go into politics?'

Juanita shrugged. 'Don't all men like that want to be a politician? His father was a state senator. Señorita Sofia is pretty, her match could help or hinder her family. Just like at my pueblo.' She tsked and shook her head. 'Poor *niña*. She won't have many choices, I'm afraid.'

'It sounds like where I come from, too. If a man isn't in

the 400, I couldn't even look at him without my mother locking me up. But we have more choices now, don't we, Juanita? We can choose who *we* like.'

Juanita flashed her a smile. 'So we can, Señora Maddie. And *your* choice right now should be dressing for dinner. Isn't Señor Gunther going to call for you soon?' She gestured to the Bakelite clock on the painted pie safe.

'Oh, yes, jeepers!' Maddie cried, and quickly covered her bowl of peeled apples before sneaking a bite into her mouth. 'We're meeting David at La Fonda.'

'Ask Dr David to lunch here soon. He works much too hard, I'm sure they don't feed him well at that boarding house.' She shook her head, thinking of David and his little room at the house behind the hospital. He was always running between there and the TB hospital out at Sunmount.

'I definitely will. He does wax rhapsodic about your lamb ragout and those tamales.'

'He's a good man, a caring man.' She nodded, and Maddie could tell Juanita was thinking about how much David helped when Juanita's husband died so horribly.

'He is a very good man. Not as handsome as Frank Altumara, though . . .'

Juanita laughed. 'Go on now with you, Señora Maddie! No more of your teasing. Francisco and I are just old friends. I could never go off to California to have a fancy actor beau.'

'Oh, I think you would be excellent in the movies yourself! Basking in the sunshine and orange groves. But I could never stand to be without you, nor Eddie and the girls. You're my family.'

'Just because there would be no more fresh apple tarts for you, since you won't learn to cook. I would take my recipe off with me to Hollywood.'

'Oh, now you're just being mean!' Maddie laughed, and hurried off to her bedroom, leaving Juanita to finish the coveted tarts.

Like all the rooms of her house, the bedroom was a small space, but very pretty, with an antique Spanish bed hand-painted with roses and ribbons, covered with a pink and white striped canopy. The same silk festooned the window and skirted her dressing table.

Behind a corner door was a rare luxury in Santa Fe – a bathroom, with a real tub and water closet, including hot and cold running water from gilded taps, laid with pink and white tiles. There was much to-do about it when she moved in, but now she noticed more and more houses had them. She was sure the Montoyas had several.

She turned on the taps and dropped in some rose-scented salts before she went back into the bedroom to change out of her beige knit day suit. Underneath she wore scandalous satin tap pants and bralette, straight from Madame Fleurie's in New York, which always made her giggle.

She stopped next to the mirrored dressing table, littered with perfume bottles and silver-backed brushes with her grandmother's monogram fading on them, which she ran through her bobbed brown hair. Her tubes of Elizabeth Arden lipstick, an enameled jewelry box – and Pete's photo in its silver frame, his blond hair pomaded flat, his smile so proud in his stiff new uniform. How different her life was now without him. What would it have been *with* him? She pressed a kiss from her fingertip to his sweet face, as she always did, and dashed back to the bathroom.

She slid so deep in the water that her head went under and she floated. How strange and perfect the world looked there, she thought whimsically. Shifting and shining. Just like the Montoyas and their perfect world. But maybe it was really the world up above the water that was upside down after all.

TWO

'*O*h, *it ain't gonna rain no more, it ain't gonna rain no more! So how you gonna wash your neck, if it ain't gonna rain no more?*'

Maddie stopped, holding on to Gunther's arm, out of breath after singing and dancing down the street. Every evening with Gunther was like a party, full of craziness and laughter, but she always felt as if she was caught up in a whirlwind storm with him.

'Oh, Gunther, darling, do stop for a moment,' she gasped, giggling. 'I'm getting too old to keep up with you and all your new music!'

'You are a veritable babe in arms, my dearest, a pearl-skinned fairy creature,' Gunther said, making sure his curling dark red hair was strictly pomaded in place, his new cravat straight. He lit one of his ever-present Gauloises and leaned against a wall to let her catch her breath. 'Tell me, how is your work progressing?'

'I'm having so much fun!' She told him about the new glass panels for La Fonda's portal, and Catalina Montoya's portrait. 'I think it's going to look quite nice.'

'She is a beautiful woman, and such lovely manners. She's what I imagine Queen Alexandra would be like, though I doubt that's true, since one reads that real royals are really so beastly rude.'

'You know her?'

'Queen Alexandra?'

Maddie laughed. 'No, silly-billy, Catalina Montoya.'

'After *Romance of the Aspen Forest* was such a hit, I was asked to be on that committee for the Indian School charity ball, she was the chairwoman.' Since Gunther's last book was a bestseller, said to be made into a movie soon, he was much in demand for local committees. 'She was no mere figurehead, either, she worked like a fiend at fundraising. I must make her a character in my next book! The sad, kind duchess.'

'Oh, yes, I remember now. You did say most of the meetings were dull as tombs.'

'Worse, darling, worse! Eternity could not be longer, all those ladies in dreadful hats arguing about decorations and napkin colors when there was real work to be done. Catalina kept them in order, though, and so sweetly. She *never* argued about anything, but kept everyone in agreement in the end. And the people-watching was quite grand.'

'But she's sad? Catalina?'

Gunther thoughtfully studied the glowing end of his Gaulois. 'Not *sad* such as most would call it. She's not La Llorona, wailing by the riverbank in her black veils. More like a – a . . .'

'A Renaissance Madonna?' Maddie said, thinking of the wistful look on Catalina's oval face as the studio window light glowed on her.

'Exactly so, darling. I knew your artist's eye would see it.'

Maybe, Maddie thought, she worried about her children and their future, just as those Botticelli Madonnas did. 'Do you know her husband?'

Gunther shook his head. 'He's not the sort for charity committees, is he, that Don Ricardo? Nor for art or literature, unless it could enrich him in some way, or give him some bragging rights, like a beautiful portrait of his beautiful wife by the finest painter in Santa Fe to hang on his wall. He's an utter businessman. His companies are the most successful in the whole state, you know, as well as the family money of the Montoyas' land grant. And you and I have both lived with men like that in our past lives.'

'Hmm, yes.' Maddie thought of her father and brother, so complacent and sure of their high place in the world, of Gunther's parents and their enormous New York department stores, their disdain for anyone not exactly like themselves. Even their own children. 'He does seldom come to Catalina's sittings, but he called for her today. He was polite, but rather brusque. Juanita said he wants to marry off his teenaged daughter to some old business acquaintance of his! And that's why he's pushing her forward during Fiesta.'

'I wouldn't be at all surprised. Sofia is such a little peach, but so quiet.' Gunther leaned closer. '*Entre nous*, Maddie darling, but a little birdie told me Sofia Montoya has been seen on the lover's lane in the foothills with a gentleman who is *not* a geriatric millionaire.'

'No!' Maddie gasped, thinking of that one little glimpse she'd had of Sofia with a blond young man. She was sure she was very lucky in her friends – Juanita knew all about the deeply rooted and entangled family connections every-where between Santa Fe and Taos, and Gunther knew all their dark little secrets. Even when she was buried in her studio, she heard all the news. It was more gossipy than her mother's 400 ever could be. 'Who was it?'

'A very spiffy, very Anglo, very Jewish lad named Jacob, or Jake, Silverstein,' Gunther whispered. He, too, was a hand-some, Anglo, Jewish lad, originally called Geoffrey, from that rich New York family of department store magnates, though he hadn't spoken of his relatives much in years. 'He is quite a successful businessman in his family's shops, very up and coming in his profession and connected to people like the Seligmans and Staabs. But of course that can't be good enough for Père Montoya. No family connections here since 1400 or whenever.'

'Does he know about Sofia and Mr Silverstein?' It was all so sad, just like a movie.

'I shouldn't think so, or she wouldn't be able to sneak out of that grand hacienda at all. She'd be locked away in a convent until she could be hustled down the cathedral aisle with her ancient suitor, and Père Montoya could find himself in a senate office.' Gunther sighed, and put out his cigarette under his polished patent shoe, which somehow never got dusty on the dirt lanes. 'That poor, sweet, pretty girl. Has her mother said anything about it?'

'Of course not. Catalina is, like you said, too regal and proper. Very friendly, though, we talk about parties and art and music, not deep, dark secrets. She did say they hoped Sofia might be La Reina at next year's Fiesta, though, so that might buy her some time. Juanita says the queen can't be engaged during her reign.'

'That's true. I'll keep my ear to the ground, darling, maybe there's some small way we could help Sofia. I should love to act as fairy godfather!' The cathedral bells suddenly rang out their stentorious notes, warning of the hour. 'We should go! You don't want to be late to meet the dishy doctor.'

They linked arms and turned toward the carved doors of La Fonda, singing very loudly, '*It's never gonna rain . . .*'

La Fonda was the most popular gathering place in Santa Fe, the most elegant, though certainly not in the stuffy New York way of Maddie's mother's pals. It was built in the style of a Spanish hacienda, surrounding an open courtyard with those glassed-in walls Maddie was helping to paint, with a large tiled fountain bubbling away at its center surrounded by metal tables and chairs where everyone took in the sun on warm days. Even now there were knots and groups of people, chatting and laughing and drinking their illicit hooch under the turquoise sky.

The corridors surrounding the courtyard were filled with beautifully carved and painted furniture cushioned with sheepskin, bright Navajo rugs softening the floors. On one side was the North Portal with its fireplace, light pouring down from the skylights between dark vigas and tea being served, and on the other was the reception desk, busy as patrons checked in for Fiesta, luggage piled everywhere. Anton, the Swiss concierge who ran the whole wild show, was smiling, shaking hands, keeping an eagle eye on everything with nary even a single dark hair out of place.

'Mrs Alwin!' he called. 'Lovely to see you. Your table is waiting.' Then he was off to mollify a matron in sable and pearls who didn't like her assigned suite. Maddie waved at him, and sent Gunther along to the restaurant to wait for her while she found the ladies' necessary.

'Miss Maddie!' Eddie called, hurrying past toward the lifts with a luggage cart. He usually worked in the dining room, but at Fiesta it was all hands on deck. Maddie marveled, as she so often did with Eddie now, at how grown-up he looked. No longer a boy, but a young man, with his blue-black hair cut short, his shoulders broad beneath his crisp white shirt. Juanita was proud, but also fretted. As Maddie did herself.

'You looking for Dr David? There he is,' Eddie said, nodding across the lobby. 'Ma says he's been working too much lately, she wants to feed him up like she does everyone else!'

Maddie glanced over to see David making his way through the streams and knots of people. She would have recognized him anywhere, in any crowd. Tall, lean, with broad shoulders under his tailored tweed jacket, light-brown, close-cropped hair just turning silvery at the temples, a short beard that emphasized his square jaw, and lips almost too pretty for his rugged looks. Several other women noticed, too, stopping their conversations to stare after him.

'He certainly *has* been working hard. They're expanding out at Sunmount, as well as his hours at the hospital,' she told Eddie. Sunmount was the TB sanatorium just outside town, an attraction for the moneyed class seeking sunshine and health. But David looked as handsome and cheerful as ever, nodding and smiling at people he knew, stopping to chat a few words. Only when he reached her side and bent his head to kiss her cheek did she glimpse a few new lines around his blue-blue eyes. He *could* use a bit of feeding up, as well as a little breakie. She wondered if they should take a jaunt out to the healing hot springs at Ojo Caliente – and book a sweet little double room at their hotel.

'You're a sight for sore eyes, Maddie,' he said, his smile widening, a dimple flashing through his golden-brown beard, newly touched with more silver.

Maddie gently touched his cheek. 'So are you. Eddie was just saying how much Juanita longs to make sure you have a good meal.'

He sighed. 'And I long to taste her tamales again. Soon, I promise. Dr McKee is back from the inoculation event at Santa Clara, then I can escape from that hospital basement for a few days.'

Maddie shivered a bit to think of that basement, which also served as the morgue. Cold, clammy, smelling of disinfectant and something stronger, metallic blood and the sweetness of decay, with those steel counters and cabinets that drained the floor. 'Juanita is making apple tarts, too, from that ever so generous crop we had from the tree. She'll save you a dozen or two.'

'And there's apple bread, and apple sauce,' Eddie said. 'I'm getting fed up with those apples!'

Maddie laughed. 'And apple brandy for the pork your uncle sent from the pueblo!'

'I would never say no to any of Juanita's pies,' David said, a blissful gleam in his eyes. Juanita's sublime cooking did that to everyone, where Maddie's burnt offerings certainly never would.

'Ed!' someone called. 'Come on, those room service trays won't deliver themselves.'

'Ah, go chase yourself!' Eddie called back. 'Gunther already went to the restaurant, Señora Maddie, holding your usual table. It's busy tonight, everyone getting ready for Fiesta. See you at home!'

David offered Maddie his arm, and they turned toward the New Mexican Restaurant behind the portal. A cheerful space, with red and turquoise tablecloths and cushioned chairs, murals on the walls painted by Olive Rush in scenes of Spanish dancers and bullfighters, it was always crowded. Today was no different.

'I was hoping we'd have a nice, quiet evening for catching up,' she said. 'But I guess that'll have to wait until after all the parties.'

'I'm looking forward to all those Fiesta plans,' David said. 'We don't have much like that in Brighton.'

'No village fetes with Morris dancers, or harvest feasts? They're going to such dos all the time in my Chesterton and Allingham books! Though someone *does* always end up murdered there, which puts a bit of a damper on the festivities.'

David laughed, a wonderful, deep rich sound that always reminded her of a fine whiskey on a cold night. 'Yes, I've been to a fete or jumble sale once or twice, luckily no dead bodies to stumble over. They're not much like Fiesta, though. Processions and costumes and burning puppets . . .'

Maddie laughed. 'And it should be even more different this

year! Thanks to Will. That old, stodgy Fiesta they tried to create these last few years, charging for tickets and all, is gone. Now it's all free and easy and fun!' They stepped into the New Mexican Room, and Maddie glimpsed a distinctive head of wild-dandelion red hair at a large round table in the middle of the space. 'And there is the man responsible himself.'

Will Shuster was waving his hands wildly as he related a tale, nearly knocking over a pottery water pitcher and making the crowd at his table duck. That was quite the usual thing with Will. His enthusiasms were stormy and loud and sudden.

'Will! Hello!' she called, waving back to him.

'Mads!' he shouted, and sent the pitcher toppling. His wife Helen, a beautiful woman with dark hair parted in the center and drawn sleekly back to reveal dangling turquoise earrings, caught it and set it right, not even pausing in her own conversation. She was used to all of it. 'Just the lady I wanted to see. I was telling everyone about our glaring gentleman friend.'

'Glaring gentleman?' David whispered. 'Is there a bad-tempered new suitor of yours I should know?'

Maddie grinned. 'Hardly. He's made of papier-mâché and cotton, or will be when we're done with him, and stuffed full of all our glooms for the year. Then we'll set him on fire.'

David's eyes widened, and he grinned. 'Sounds the bee's knees to me. No more glooms, I say! Bright skies ahead!'

And that's exactly what David deserved. After his work in the war, the terrible death of his wife, he deserved so much happiness. 'That's what we have here, of course. Endless blue skies.' Maddie thought of her trays and trays of blue tubes of paint, and no shade ever quite captured the enchanting turquoise and azure expanse. 'I always look forward to Will's party schemes. Remember that circus fete? But this one does mean more work for me.'

'I'll leave you to it for the moment, then, love, and join Gunther. He said he'll tell me about the newest murder in his current book, I'm meant to help with the angle of knife wounds.'

Maddie laughed. 'I do enjoy a man who knows about knife-wound angles. Be there in a jiffy.' She kissed his cheek and hurried across the restaurant, dodging around the packed tables.

Will's table was crowded as always, with too few chairs for too many people, but everyone cheerfully squashed up as Maddie joined them. John Sloan, one of the most venerable of the local artists, and his hard-drinking wife Dolly; Fremont Ellis, who did gorgeous landscapes, and his beautiful local wife Laurencita; Will's friends, the 'Cinco Pintores' artists who all lived near him on Monte Sol; Dana Johnson, a local newspaper editor who had first named Zozobra; the Hendersons, local patrons of the arts; Gustav Baumann, who had created fits with making Zozo's head first too small then too large. They were all there, talking over each other, arguing, laughing.

Helen Shuster poured Maddie a drink from the rescued pitcher, and Will showed her a sketch on a napkin. Maddie sighed as she thought of how irate the impeccable Anton would be to see his linens ruined again.

'I was just showing everyone how Mr Zozobra will look once he's finished,' Will said. Dana had called their old man Zozobra after the Spanish for 'worry', which they would banish. 'Gus finally has the head the right size. Hopefully, if it all works according to plan, we can go bigger next year. Twenty feet! Fifty!'

'Bigger will never fit in our garden,' Helen said.

'Then we'll move it!' Will declared. 'To the mountains, maybe. He can go sixty feet out there, if we find a good valley, not just six. If it works, which it's sure to. There will be fireworks! Orchestras! Dancers!'

Maddie studied the people around the table, all of them offering their opinions on the celebration. She knew most of them, of course. One of them, though, was a new face. An older man, tall and thin, craggy in his face and sun-browned, but handsome, with the sculpted cheekbones of a Renaissance saint. His jacket was worn at the elbows, his cuffs stained with paint, so he fit right in.

'Hello,' she said, offering her hand. 'I'm Madeline Alwin. You must be new in Santa Fe.'

'Oh, yes, I must remember my manners, as Helen always tells me,' Will said. 'Mads, this is Paul Vynne. An artist, naturally, or he wouldn't be here with us crazy lot. I knew him back in Pennsylvania when I was a young man. We both studied with the famous Herr Rotheim. Paul's traveling the country, working on some marvelous scenes for the railroad company, which is paying him an absolute fortune. I hate him for that, I must say!'

'How fascinating!' Maddie said. 'I'd love to see more of the country, but I also can't bear to leave home here.'

'I understand that, it's incredible, your deserts and mountains. My dearest art teacher, Herr Rotheim, teaches in Albuquerque now and I hope to meet up with him.' Paul smiled and shook her hand, his fingers stained with more paint, rough at the edges, but strong. 'But is it fascinating that I'm an artist, or that I've managed to put up with Will for all these years?'

Maddie laughed. 'Both. I'm something of an artist myself, and I would love to hear more about your work with the railroads. I know Couse does that, and Hemings.'

'Something of an artist! Maddie is too modest,' Will said. 'She's one of our most talented colorists! You two have that in common. And Paul is a wizard with a boar's hair brush, such texture.'

'It seems like I've arrived just in time for all the fun,' Paul said. 'Your Fiesta!'

'It's usually rather quiet, but thanks to Will there's more happening this year. Parades and dances, and Zozobra, of course,' Maddie answered. She did like this old friend of Will's, with his friendly, enthusiastic smile, his interest in their little town 'If you're still around, though, you're sure to be put to work.'

'I look forward to it. My fingers get itchy when they're not holding a paintbrush,' Paul said.

'We shall put you to work, then, Paul!' Will declared. 'Santa Fe is a place that keeps pace with the sun and moon, and not the clock! It's easy to be a bohemian here, to enjoy life on its own terms, as you should, my friend. We can look at the world and give back to it creatively!'

Another group came into the restaurant, and Maddie saw it was Catalina Montoya, dressed in a navy and white knit Chanel suit, her dark hair shining under a feathered cloche hat. She held on to the arm of a man, tall, silver-haired, as well dressed as she was, smiling down at her gently from beneath a close-trimmed mustache. Juan-Antonio, her son, trailed behind them, seeming rather bored by it all, as young men were often wont to do. But Catalina and her companion took no notice, so deep in conversation were they.

'She's a looker,' Paul said. But his gaze as he examined Catalina was that of an appraising artist, not an admiring man. As if he imagined how to paint her hair, her shoulders, the sad curve of her smile.

'That's Catalina Montoya,' Maddie said. 'I'm painting her portrait right now, she's quite a wonderful model.'

Paul looked startled. 'Montoya?'

'Wife of Don Ricardo Montoya, one of our most wealthy businessmen in Santa Fe. And she was a Gomez before she married, they came here with Don Diego de Vargas himself,' Will said. 'The young man is her son, Juan-Antonio. His father wants him to join the family business after he goes to Harvard, but I hear he wants to be an artist, just as any right-thinking person would. Not sure about the other man with them . . .'

He looked rather disgruntled he didn't know *everyone* on sight.

'That's André Fernandez,' William Henderson said. 'A rancher out in Rio Arriba County, though his family is from Santa Fe. He doesn't come to town often now, he must be here for Fiesta.'

'They do seem friendly,' Will said, and Maddie noticed how Señor Fernandez leaned close to Catalina as he held out her chair, making her smile up at him gently. 'It's nice to see Señora Montoya out and about, she usually just attends private parties or meetings of the Sociedad Folklórica.'

'Have she and her husband always lived in Santa Fe?' Paul asked quietly.

'Oh, yes. The Montoyas and Gomezes are quite ancient,' Alice Henderson said. 'But I do think Don Ricardo went off to university somewhere else when he was young, ages ago. Yale or something. Wherever it was, he seemed to have learned a lot. He grew his family business by leaps and bounds.'

'Marrying a Gomez didn't hurt,' Dana said.

As if summoned by the sound of his name, though the restaurant was too loud for eavesdropping, Señor Fernandez rose from his table and made his way across the room, stopping to talk to a few people until he reached Will's group. 'William Henderson! It has been much too long.' Up close, he was even more handsome, the silver of his hair shimmering, his eyes a distinctive hazel, his smile unforced and friendly.

'Indeed. Are you here in Santa Fe long, André?' William asked.

'For Fiesta. I was asked to chair the planning committee for the masquerade ball here at La Fonda, as my father once did. I'm very glad to be here again, and see my old chums,' André answered, with a flash of a quick smile to Catalina's table. 'Do introduce me to everyone. I love meeting new friends.'

After the introductions were made, Maddie excused herself to make her way to her own table, the same one she always sat at in a quiet corner beneath the Spanish dancers mural, where Gunther and David were in animated conversation over some aspect of knife blades. Maddie noticed Catalina and Juan-Antonio seemed to be arguing about something, whispering with a worried look on Catalina's face and anger on Juan-Antonio's. As Maddie passed them, though, Catalina quickly covered her worried expression with a smile, and waved. Juan-Antonio took a deep drink from a teacup Maddie was sure did not contain tea.

'You two do seem to be having fun without me,' Maddie said as she slipped into the chair next to David's. Gunther poured her her own teacup of Orange Blossom.

'Never, darling. The world is gray and dull without you,' Gunther said. 'We were talking about daggers and such. But who was Will's lovely new friend? So divine-looking with that widow's peak, like Valentino!'

'Paul Vynne. He's an artist, it seems Will knew him back in Pennsylvania, and now he's traveling the country painting scenes for the railroad.'

'I do hope he might stay for a while,' Gunther said wistfully. 'This town could use some new faces.'

'It's always nice to hear some fresh gossip, true,' Maddie said. 'But remember what happened last time there were "new faces" with the movie people! There was *actual* blood.'

Gunther waved that away. 'Oh, yes, that murder bit was

certainly wretched. The movie stars, though, quite, quite divine. Did you see Rex Neville is a great sensation in German films now?

'Well, it *did* set my cousin Gwen back on her career course,' Maddie said. Gwen was on the New York stage right now, getting excellent notices as Hero in a new production of *Much Ado*. 'I wouldn't like to see it happen again, though.'

'I'm sure we shan't,' Gunther declared. 'What can go wrong with Fiesta? Parties galore, everyone having fun . . .'

'And La Conquistadora watching over it all,' Maddie said, thinking of the wooden statue of the Madonna the Spanish had brought back with them after the Revolt, the statue Don Diego himself prayed to and promised her a celebration every year. She had the most divine wardrobe now, hundreds of little gowns she wore on her Fiesta processions. 'I'm sure you're right. We all deserve some fun. Especially you, David darling, you really have been working so hard. Tell us what's been happening.'

'Yes, I want all the gory details,' Gunther said. 'I could use them all in my new novel! I want to make it all feel so authentic.'

David laughed, and Maddie was happy to see he did look more relaxed, more at ease. 'I'm not sure how *gory* it's been lately, lucky for me, but there was this one case . . .'

As David told them about his newest patients, their dinners arrived, La Fonda's famous Pollo Lucreccio, chicken with a sauce of chile, cumin and oregano found nowhere else. The time flew past, as it always did when Maddie was with her favorite people in her favorite place. When the coffee was brought, she was surprised to see André Fernandez walking right toward their table.

'Mrs Vaughn-Alwin, yes?' he said, with an actual little courtly bow, like he was Francis Drake. 'Are you perhaps related to Henry Vaughn?'

Maddie was surprised. 'Why, yes. He's my brother. I didn't realize anyone here had heard of him!'

He smiled, and Maddie saw Gunther was quite right – he looked quite like a slightly older Valentino, with such a lovely smile. No wonder Catalina looked so at ease with him. He was a much easier presence than Ricardo. 'He has done a bit of work for my family when he had contacts in the East. I am André Fernandez.'

'Yes, Señora Montoya's friend.'

'Indeed! Our families have known each other since we were children. It is she who suggested your artistic talents might be just what I need right now.'

'I'm intrigued, and flattered she would say so. How can I help?'

'I am choosing the committee for the masquerade ball, as I told Señor Shuster. It's been a long time since I was involved in any Fiesta events, but it was once my father's task and I'm happy to try it myself. I have to live up to his fine reputation. The problem is I am afraid I have no artistic talent myself, and we need advice for some of the decorations to make them distinctive. Catalina tells me you are a great talent indeed, and I have always trusted her fine taste. It would be very last minute indeed, I'm afraid, but any help you could offer would be so appreciated.'

'That's most kind of her! But it's easy with a model like her.' She thought quickly, calculating how many people would be on the committee who would need portraits painted. 'I would love to help if I can. And if you also need a writer, this is my friend Gunther Ryder, a best-selling novelist. And Dr David Cole.' She made the introductions, and glanced at Gunther, who gave her an encouraging nod.

'I am so happy you can help us, Señora Vaughn-Alwin. We are having a small committee meeting here at La Fonda tomorrow, if it would be convenient for you to join us.'

'I will be there, thank you,' Maddie said, and Señor Fernandez took his leave with another courtly bow.

'You're very popular, my dearest,' Gunther said. 'A masquerade ball!'

'It should be very interesting,' Maddie said. 'And I doubt there can be any bloodshed at a Fiesta committee . . .'

As Maddie walked home happily hand-in-hand with David, chatting companionably about her paintings in progress, his hospital shifts, and Fiesta, she took a deep breath of the breeze that smelled deliciously of piñon and roasting chiles, of fresh rain on the way. She heard the music from the plaza, and smiled.

'What a lovely evening,' she said, and leaned her head on David's shoulder. The distant mountains looked like blue-purple shadows against the sunset, bright sprays of coral and pink light bursting out from behind them before the glow vanished and stars blinked on.

The glowing light made everything around them golden as well, pale yellow and delicate shell-pink on the adobe walls, shot through with veins of darker charcoal-gray. Scarlet-tipped leaves trembled in the breeze, delicate against the hardier, scrubby-green chamisa. Every day, every evening had scenes she longed to paint, a world she wanted to wrap up in and vanish.

A world she shared with someone else now. She peeked up at David, and saw him watching her in return, his blue eyes glowing and intense, as if he could look right into her very thoughts. The gold flecks in their depth made him seem like a sunrise all in himself. It made her feel warm all over, safe – things she'd never thought to feel again after her husband died. But life was all new again.

'With all your Fiesta gadding about, you'll probably be too busy for me,' he teased.

'Oh, I dare say between your healing everyone in town and me painting every surface in sight, we'll muddle through somehow,' she answered.

She closed her eyes, and went up on tiptoe to kiss him. His lips caressed hers, making her melt with a rising urgency. Yes, there was safety as well as fire in that touch, and she felt like the luckiest dame in the whole country in that moment.

Fireworks suddenly shot off above their heads, exploding into the darkening sky in sparkling reds, greens, blues, silvers. She laughed and snuggled close to him, sure that nothing could harm them now.

THREE

I t was the teeniest bit late when Maddie tumbled out of her bedroom the next morning, but the house smelled deliciously of fresh coffee and sizzling bacon, along with the crisp, pine-scented breeze from the open windows and Juanita's own recipe of lemon polish. Juanita was at the stove, humming as she cooked, while the dogs lounged hopefully at her feet.

'Extra-strong coffee, Señora Maddie, and the dairy just delivered some cream,' she said with a knowing smile. She knew just what Maddie needed after a late evening with her friends at La Fonda.

'Juanita, you are the veriest angel,' Maddie sighed, and gratefully poured herself a large mug of the dark brew before sitting down at the scrubbed kitchen table to flip through the newspaper. Pigs escaped, a new Chinese restaurant opening, a young wife who ran away but came back again. Fiesta happenings.

Juanita cracked some eggs with a flick of her wrist. 'How was Dr David?'

'Very well, looking forward to some of your cooking! We'll have a dinner very soon. I haven't seen Father Malone in an age, either.' Father Malone was at the cathedral, an Irishman who loved a good Chesterton novel as much as Maddie did.

'I saw him at confession yesterday, he's busy getting ready for the Fiesta processions. They were roasting green chiles at Kaune's grocery, too,' Juanita said. 'I can make some enchiladas, or maybe a lamb stew. Was anyone else interesting at the restaurant?'

'Oodles of people. The Hendersons, the Sloans. Will Shuster, of course wildly enthusiastic about his Zozobra pageant. He has so many plans for it all!'

'Hmm,' Juanita said with a doubtful frown.

'You aren't looking forward to it all, Juanita? It sounds so jolly. The Hysterical Parade, dances . . .'

Juanita took butter from the icebox. 'Once it was all about quiet family things, Masses and processions. I liked that. But anything that brings people together is a good idea, I'm sure. Santa Fe can be *too* quiet sometimes, can't it?'

Quiet was exactly what Maddie needed after Pete died in the war, when she felt so lost, stumbling along a dark tunnel where she didn't know which end was up or down. She still relished the peace, the history of the town, the time to paint and think, to look at the mountains, to just *be*. It was the great gift of finding her true home at last. Now, though, as time worked its magic and she found her own joy again, she found she liked being around people, having good friends, people who let her be herself.

'I do enjoy seeing everyone I love come together,' she said, spreading the butter on her toast. She slipped a bite to the dogs. 'Like you, and the children, and Gunther . . .'

Juanita gave her a small, knowing smile. 'Like Dr David?'

Maddie felt her cheeks turn hot, and she quickly took another gulp of coffee. 'I – I'm not sure. Maybe. Probably. I don't know! I used to leap into emotions so fast, but after Pete . . .'

'I understand.' Juanita nodded, her smile turning a bit sad. 'After my husband, I can't imagine opening myself to such things again. Not with the children still here to keep safe. It's not a bad thing Francisco is so far away, maybe.'

Maddie gave her a teasing nudge across the table. 'But you do have his lovely letters!'

Juanita even laughed, a rare event. 'They are not so terrible to get in the mail, true. Your Dr David, though, is right here. And I can see he cares about you so much. He's a fine man, a caring man, not like my husband was.'

'And I care about him! So much. I can't imagine what things would be like without him now.' And she really couldn't. Seeing David, being with him, talking to him, kissing him – it made everything sunnier. Yet just like her, he had known such loss, with the death of his wife.

'Things are so nice the way they are,' Maddie said. 'I guess I'm just a bit of a fraidy-cat now. Scared of change.'

'It's frightening, for sure. But the world, our lives, they always change. Even love, when it looks like it will always be the same.'

'Just like Fiesta changes?'

'Just like that. It's not all bad.'

'I was asked to give some artistic advice to the masquerade ball committee, by one of Catalina Montoya's friends,' Maddie said. 'Perhaps I should tell them not to change too much!'

'It is an honor to be on such a committee, though, Señora Maddie!' Juanita said, slipping the dogs some toast of her own. 'Especially since you haven't been here very long.'

Maddie nodded, thinking of how small Santa Fe could really be, how the different groups kept to themselves. Quite insular, really. Much like Manhattan. 'I know. I'm such a greenhorn!'

'But you seem as if you've been here forever,' Juanita said soothingly, if not entirely convincingly. 'Who asked you about the committee?'

'André Fernandez. Do you know him? I saw him at La Fonda last night, with Catalina and her son Juan-Antonio.'

'Everyone knows of Señor Fernandez! His ranch is one of the largest in Rio Arriba County. I'm surprised you haven't met him before, though he seldom comes to town these days, I think. He supplies most of our beef. It's always the best quality.'

'I doubt we run in the same circles at all.' Maddie's artistic friends and people like the Fernandezes and Montoyas, old families, seldom mixed a lot. Just like her parents and their Knickerbocker circles. 'He did seem quite nice, and very solicitous of Catalina. Gunther thinks he looks like Valentino.'

'Their families have always lived near each other. Though the Gomezes are very old, even more than the Montoyas or the Fernandezes. I think I heard they were meant to be engaged once, but that was a very long time ago, I was still a girl at the pueblo then.'

'Fascinating! I wonder what happened. It's like a Jane Austen novel. This might as well be Highbury!'

'I am surprised Juan-Antonio was with his mother, though,' Juanita said, with a disapproving little click of her tongue.

'It's true he didn't look very happy to be there,' Maddie said. 'In fact . . .'

She couldn't say more, as the twins came running into the kitchen in a whirlwind of noise and hair ribbons and their school-uniform white pinafores. The dogs went into a frenzy of barking, dashing around them.

'Señora Maddie, you said you'd walk with us to school today,' Pearl said, snatching a bit of bacon from the table.

'You promised,' said Ruby.

'Of course I will!' Maddie said, giving them such tight hugs they squirmed and giggled. It made her sad to think they would soon be much too big to want her to walk with them. 'Don't I walk with you every week on this day?' And stopped at the candy store for a secret visit.

'You won't be going anywhere at all, my wild *niña* monkeys, with your hair in such a state,' Juanita scolded, kissing their rosy cheeks before she put bowls of oatmeal in front of them. 'Brushes, now, and proper bows with your ribbons, *hijas*! And no pestering Señora Maddie for lemon drops . . .'

The twins chattered happily as Maddie walked them to school through the streets just stirring to life for the day. A few cars rattled past, throwing up dust, though none as fancy as Ricardo Montoya's or as sporty as Gunther's Duesenberg; it was still mostly horses and donkeys and carts. Shop doors were opening, window shutters unlatching, wagons full of groceries being delivered from Kaune's and the dairy. The candy store was their very first stop.

'Is there really going to be a parade for pets again?' Ruby said, examining the bag of lemon drops for the best one.

'Yes, the Desfile de los Niños,' Maddie answered, and took Pearl's hand to draw her away from the distraction of a milliner's window. Pearl already loved fashion. 'It's for all the children in town to show off their dogs and cats.'

'What if the pet is a guinea pig, or a turtle?' Ruby said.

'Or a badger!' added Pearl.

Ruby scoffed. 'No one has a pet badger! They're too mean.'

'Well, some day, when I'm a veterinarian, I'll tame a badger and have one as *my* pet,' Pearl declared.

Ruby frowned doubtfully. 'How can you be a veterinarian? You're a *girl*.'

'It's the 1920s, my darlings,' Maddie answered them. She thought of when she was their age, fastened tightly into her starched ruffles and buttoned boots, with one thing expected of her one day – to marry properly. She wanted so much more for these lovely girls. 'You can do whatever you like, if you go about it right. And we definitely need more veterinarians around here, with all those ranchers and so many people with their non-badger pets.' They each took one of her hands and swung around the corner, past Kaune's and toward the school. 'What are you going to do, then, Ruby dear?'

Ruby looked thoughtful. 'Be a mother, I guess. Or a nun, like Sister Mary Cecilia! She knows ever so much. Then I could teach *lots* of children.'

'That's super-boring,' Pearl said.

Ruby gave her twin a little shove with her free hand. 'It's not boring at all! You just have no imagination. The sisters are always busy! Teaching, praying, visiting the sick, playing football in the convent garden . . .'

'No squabbling, girls,' Maddie insisted, squeezing their hands. 'We're almost where Sister Mary Cecilia herself can see you, and you don't want a bad mark against your behavior to get back to your mother.'

That settled them right down, as Juanita brooked no bad manners. The school was within sight now, with its cream-colored stone walls and gray slate mansard roof in the French style that stood out from all the tan and pale-pink adobe. The chapel next to it rose up like a jewel box, stained glass and gray walls, with a statue of Mary high on her steeple, peering down at the passers-by.

'But we *can* go to the parade, right, Señora Maddie?' Pearl said. 'And take Buttercup and Pansy?'

'Yes, of course, if you mind your manners. We'll have to come up with some clever costumes, and win the prize!' Maddie slipped them the last of the lemon drops and sent them up the polished stone steps to the school doors, waving

at Sister Mary Cecilia. She remembered hearing that the sister
had also taught Sofia Montoya, and wondered if the twins
were as well regarded there as Sofia seemed to have been.

Maddie turned toward La Fonda again, where Señor
Fernandez's committee meeting was being held, and popped
one of the tart candies into her mouth. It was a beautiful
autumn day, the trees starting to turn golden and scarlet at the
tips, the sun shimmering through them, children kicking at
the piles of leaves just starting to tumble to the walkway,
couples strolling arm-in-arm. Maddie studied them, but none
were Sofia or Jake Silverstein.

She reached for the heavy brass handle of the carved hotel
doors, and heard the crunch of a car's tires coming up San
Francisco Street, the tourist van that brought passengers from
the train station a few miles away in Lamy. The cathedral bells
rang out the hour just a block away, and she hurried her steps,
remembering the time. It would never do to be late for her
first meeting!

'Good morning, Mrs Alwin,' Anton greeted her from behind
the reception desk. It was quieter at the hotel than when she
usually visited, but still steadily humming, a tour group gathering at the reception desk to board the van to one of the
pueblos.

'Good morning, Anton,' Maddie said, taking off her gloves
and making sure her hat was straight and the embroidered
sage-green coat that matched her new crepe day dress was
smooth. 'Are you *always* on duty here, then? Golly!'

He laughed, and pushed his glasses up his nose. 'Almost
always. But there is constantly something interesting happening,
I must say, and it's good to keep my eye on it all. Your
committee meeting is in the Terraza Room.' One of the most
elegant meeting rooms in the hotel, Maddie remembered, with
its skylights and European chandeliers.

Most of the committee seemed to already be there when
she stepped inside. A long blue damask-draped table was laid
with folders and sketches, luxurious red-upholstered armchairs
drawn around. Portraits studied them curiously from their
gilded frames, people who had surely once run the Fiesta
committees in their own days.

And they were probably ancestors of some of the committee members there right now. She nodded at a few people she knew, Mrs Vasquez and Señor and Señora Otero. Mostly old Santa Fe families, but Alice Henderson, a poet and influential society lady of Santa Fe, pretty and dark-haired in a lovely red velvet coat and hat, waved at her happily.

'Ah, Señora Vaughn-Alwin,' André Fernandez said with one of his gallant bows. 'We are so happy you agreed to join us last minute! Do have a seat here next to me.'

As Maddie took the offered chair, Alice said, 'Yes, we were thrilled you agreed to help us, Maddie. We're so sadly unoriginal when it comes to decorations, and my husband didn't have time for us today. We only have a vague theme of "Old Seville". What do you think of these drawings?'

Maddie studied the ideas, lots of papier-mâché balconies and bright tissue flowers, as one would expect from 'Old Seville', but she was sure they could add more oomph. She thought of an 'Under the Sea Baile' Will Shuster had organized last year right here in La Fonda, all blue silk draperies and partygoers dressed as sharks and mermaids. It had all gone a bit wonky when someone knocked over a giant lobster and destroyed one of the hotel's beautiful silver lamps, but surely this party needn't go quite so far as *that*.

'What about something like – this?' She quickly sketched out a few ideas of her own, just a few small touches to make the scene more 1920s-modern. A few people tsked and frowned, murmuring about 'tradition', but several nodded enthusiastically, and Maddie set about a more detailed drawing.

The lady who sat next to her, tall and elegant in a fur-collared coat and ruby earrings, turned to her and said, 'You are painting Catalina Montoya's portrait, are you not, Mrs Alwin?'

'Yes, I am.'

'You must have some talent then.' She sounded a bit doubtful.

Maddie tried not to laugh. 'I suppose I do. But Mrs Montoya makes it a very easy task.'

'Yes, and she and I are old friends. I am Maria Gutierrez, I usually live in Nambe these days but I couldn't miss Fiesta. I was at Loretto with Catalina when we were girls. We thought

she would marry a prince back then, she was so beautiful!'
Mrs Gutierrez reached for one of the cut-glass water goblets
on the table, her pink-painted lips wistfully downturned. 'Such
silly girls we were. Her family meant her for Ricardo Montoya
all along. Just as my parents meant me for my husband.'

'Don't mention Montoya's name near me again!' Señor
Otero said darkly, crossing his arms in his pin-striped suit. His
earlier genial smile was vanished, replaced with dark clouds.

'Ricardo Montoya?' Mrs Gutierrez said, befuddled. 'Wh
– why not? He is from one of our finest families, we have
known him for ages.'

'You mean your husband has said nothing to you?' someone
else said.

'Said what?' Mrs Gutierrez asked.

Maddie glanced around the table, taking in red cheeks,
averted gazes.

'Montoya has been handing out bad business advice,' Mr
Otero said brusquely.

'That can't be!' Mrs Gutierrez cried. 'He would never . . .'

'My dear friends,' André Fernandez said softly, gently. 'We
have much work to do today. And no time for such specula-
tion, it has no place here. Wouldn't you agree, Mateo?'

Mr Otero folded his arms tighter, but finally nodded. 'Of
course, André. Merely a little word of warning among, as you
say, dear friends. Some people are never what they appear.
But yes, we should finalize this menu . . .'

FOUR

Will Shuster's back garden of his house on Camino del Monte Sol was large and tangled with vegetable patches and scrubby chamisa blooming yellow at the tips, windswept and dusty, but the sun was warm and crispy-golden on the autumn trees, the sky a limitless brilliant blue with a few cottony puffs of clouds drifting past as it stretched overhead to the dark gray, always-watching mountains in the distance. It was a fine day to be working outside with friends.

Will's house was small and rambling, like the other haphazard dwellings along Monte Sol, which had become an unofficial artists' barrio. His original two rooms, with their small, low windows and old vigas, had grown with the appearance of his children, with new rooms sticking off at angles and a screened porch and studio. Unlike Maddie's house on Canyon Road, it offered sweeping views to the mountains on either horizon. And there was always room for friends, with a guest casita up a slope on one side, large tubs of water lined up along either side waiting for the Zozobra conflagration. Maddie had heard Paul Vynne was staying there right now.

They were building Will's new creation, that Zozobra, on a rise above the back portal where he could be seen for miles once he was set alight. Crowds scurried around, offering advice, adding little flourishes to the Old Man Gloom, laughing and larking about. Children and dogs ran free.

The little hacienda was bursting with activity today, as it was most days. Will believed fervently in the freedom of artistry they had all found there, the place to let those free spirits roam. It was easy to enjoy life there at his place.

Perched on a stepladder, Maddie added a ring of bright

green paint around Zozo's enormous round dark eyes, giving
him even more of an air of malevolence.

'What do you think?' she asked Olive Rush, who worked
on Zozo's long white skirt. Her own pleated velvet Navajo
skirt was covered with a paint-speckled smock, the ever-present
turban on her hair slipping over her eyes.

'I wouldn't want to see him coming toward me in a dark
alley at night!'

Maddie flicked at one of his long hands, the pointed finger-
nails painted red. They would wave in the air as he went up
in flames. 'Ugh! A demon zombie. Just like that scary German
movie, the one about the clay giant that comes to life and
stomps around the town.'

'That's why we're going to turn him to ash!' Will declared
from atop the rickety ladder where he made the crimson of
Zozo's hair. 'Send him into the ether with all our worries so
we'll have a bright new year.'

'And sell lots of paintings,' Fremont Ellis, one of Will's
coterie of artists known as the Cinco Pintores, said, wildly
waving his brush.

Paul, Will's visiting friend, held up a box filled with slips
of paper, scribbled over in many handwritings. 'What are
these?'

'Our glooms, of course!' Will said, turning to take the
box. 'I've had everyone write down their worries and cares,
and we'll put them inside our demonic gentleman here to
turn into smoke. They'll float up into the sky, and – poof!
Begone.'

'And that is why he is called Zozobra?' Paul asked.

'Hopefully, he'll be something of a hit, and we'll do it again
next year. Bigger and more spectacular!' Will fondly patted
the papier-mâché arm, designed to flail in dudgeon when it
caught fire.

'He seems tall enough now to me,' Helen said doubtfully.
'I gave up my dahlias so he would have room!'

'Six feet is nothing for getting rid of our worries! He should
be twenty, fifty feet. A hundred! And we'll find him a better
place next year, where he can really spread out.' In his enthu-
siasm, Will almost tumbled off the ladder. 'He is really quite

flammable. I hadn't really considered that. We'll need bigger tubs of water out by Paul's casita.' Will's schemes usually didn't involve much forethought. But they generally worked out well.

'I'll put out more water buckets,' Helen fretted. 'And make sure the children don't get too close.'

'They'll love it!' Will said. He called to the racing gang of kids nearby, his own and several others, 'What say you, children?'

'Burn him, burn him! *Viva la fiesta!*' they shouted.

'Exactly,' Will said. 'Can you do – something with the eyes, Mads? Make them more evil?'

'More evil. Absolutely.' Maddie frowned as she thought of the evil she'd seen in the last few years, murders and bootleggers and blackmailers. Juanita's husband murdered in an alley behind La Fonda; the murder at the movie set. All the people who could have done the deeds.

In the gravel circle in front of the little house, a yellow Hispano Suiza squealed to a stop, tossing up a dusty plume. A tall, dark-haired woman dressed in a floral chiffon dress and matching wide-brimmed hat, spectacular pearls around her neck, climbed down. Maddie saw it was Elizabeth White, one of the wealthy White sisters, with two of her enormous prize-winning wolfhounds barking from the back seat.

The Whites had been at Santa Fe for many years, building up their grand estate El Delirio; she'd heard they stopped there on their way to California from Philadelphia to get their hair done, and liked it so much they never moved on. William Henderson had designed their house, one that Maddie quite envied, though she could never have kept up such a place, complete with tennis courts and dog kennels and art studios.

'Helllooo, Will darling!' Elizabeth called, standing up on the running board to wave her large straw hat. The pink chiffon scarf tied around it caught in the wind like a banner, and the light gleamed on her triple strand of pearls. 'And Madeline Alwin! We haven't seen you at El Delirio in an age.'

'No, and you promised me a game on those new tennis courts of yours,' Maddie called back with a laugh.

'We thought you were all closed up for parties this year,'
Will said. 'We haven't seen you or Martha all summer!'
    Elizabeth laughed, free and raucous. 'We were at dog shows
back East. But who can live without parties? I'm not ready to
go live in a cave like your friend Mr Sloan; living for art is
all well and good but we need *fun*, too.' She reached through
the open car window to ruffle the head of one of the dogs who
drooled against her. 'I came to say hello to your guest. Hi
there, Paul!'
    Paul grinned back, and waved. 'Hello, there, Elizabeth!'
    'Where did you two meet?' Will asked, wiping his paintbrush
on his denim pants and making his wife frown.
    'I found him wandering yesterday like a little lost lamb
down Garcia Street, just past the house, and found out he
knows everything about tennis as well as art. He said he's a
friend of yours!'
    'I admit I can be a shameless name-dropper sometimes,'
Paul said cheerfully.
    'I do claim him, I'm afraid,' Will said. 'I didn't know he
was in Santa Fe to shirk his work by wandering down Garcia,
though!'
    Elizabeth shaded her eyes to study Zozo. 'He's coming
along well, isn't he? Quite fearsome. I love it. Perfect way to
kick off Fiesta, isn't he? We'll all be busy with your new
plans.'
    'Maddie here just got put on the masquerade ball
committee,' Will said.
    Elizabeth turned her piercing gaze on to Maddie. 'You poor
lamb! Better to stay under this town's scope, and avoid all
such dull, daft things and stick to Zozobra.' Not that the White
sisters were ever 'under the scope' of anyone. Their house at
El Delirio, 'the Madness', was vast, and they had parties there
all the time. Parties were constant among their artistic circles,
parties to celebrate birthdays, sunny afternoons, selling a
painting, finishing a painting, being sad because the last party
was too long ago. 'But André *is* a darling, you'll be able to
do just as you like. Not like working on committees with
Ricardo Montoya.' She shuddered in her silk frock. 'What a
taskmaster he is! So dull.'

'Will here is really the taskmaster,' Maddie said. 'Driving us all to finish his Frankenstein's Monster!'

'And no gin for any of you until that papier-mâché is dry,' Will scolded. 'You lot drink me out of house and home!'

'Well, you all deserve a respite!' Elizabeth said. 'Come to El Delirio tomorrow, we're having a tiny soiree to show off our new swimming pool. Another masquerade party, Mayan themed! No working for your gin, I promise! Just be sure and wear a costume.'

And it would be no cheap bathtub gin there, either, Maddie was sure. El Delirio parties only featured the best French champagne. And it was never a 'small soiree'. It always involved almost the whole town! And any strays the sisters found, like Paul Vynne.

'I did already ask this darling Paulie, and he agreed,' Elizabeth said, flirtatiously waggling her fingers at him.

He grinned. 'I do want to learn everything about this lovely town of yours, Will. You've been keeping it from your old friends too long!'

'It's hardly hidden, Paul, you're just too itchy-footed to stop anywhere for more than five minutes,' Will said.

'I'm not sure I'll move on again now,' Paul said. 'I seem to have found just what I've been looking for.'

'I do hope so, darling.' Elizabeth climbed back behind the wheel, and waved at them with a flash of her emerald and amethyst rings. 'See you all then! Don't forget – costumes.'

As she roared away, Will dashed off to take care of some new painting emergency, and Paul and Maddie strolled back to where Zozo waited, swaying in the breeze from the cord that held him tethered to his stake.

'She's quite a . . .' Paul said, looking doubtful.

Maddie laughed. 'Force of nature?'

'Yeah, you could say that.'

'She and her sister Martha are great patrons of the arts here, and inveterate party-givers. But generous and kind. Martha is quieter, more delicate, but she still enjoys a good party. Wait'll you see inside their house! It's incredible. Modeled after Laguna Pueblo, they say, and named after a bar they liked in Seville.'

'This whole town seems like a force of nature. I can see how Will was always much too big for Pennsylvania. This place suits him.'

'I can't imagine Santa Fe without him. We do adore him here!'

'You seem to belong here, too.'

Maddie gazed up into the sky, that endless expanse that was constantly changing, constantly dramatic or peaceful or serene or melancholy. 'I hope so. I never felt so much like myself until I came here.'

He smiled sadly. 'I don't think I've *ever* quite felt like myself. Except maybe for a brief while, a very long time ago.'

Maddie gave him a sympathetic smile. She did understand that feeling so well. 'How so, Mr Vynne?'

That sadness floated away, like those puffs of clouds, and he smiled. 'Oh, call me Paul, please. Any friend of Will's I hope can be mine, too!'

'That's one of the magical things about Santa Fe, you'll find,' Maddie said. 'You can put the past on the far side of the mountains and leave it there! Pain and heartache, all forgotten. Dissolved into this sky.'

Paul smiled wryly as he tipped back his head to look up into that sky, changed to a deeper azure now. It changed in an instant, always; mauve, gold, lavender, orange, rose. 'It certainly seems big enough to hold it all. And it never comes back to haunt you?'

'Well, sometimes,' she admitted. 'In the middle of the night. I guess our old loves don't just vanish altogether from our hearts. But life does get brighter. Holds out new purposes. Like art!'

'I do hope so.' He pulled out some sketches from a portfolio he'd lodged on the porch, and showed her the images. They were quick charcoal studies, houses near El Delirio, towering old cottonwoods, children skipping rope, dogs snoozing in the shade. They were wonderful, filled with movement and emotion. He'd obviously not just been 'loafing' up on Garcia Street. 'I did get the sense from Miss White that a person can't *totally* leave the past behind, though. Old families, old manners . . .'

'Well – yes, there is that, too,' Maddie said. 'I doubt humans could eradicate all snobbery no matter what they do! There has to be a *the* Mrs Astor everywhere.'

'And who would you say is *the* Mrs Astor here? I saw that beauty Mrs Montoya at La Fonda, and Miss White said her family was quite ancient.'

'Yes, Catalina Montoya is very ladylike. But she'd be no good at running a town with an Astor-like fist. She just doesn't seem to care enough, aristocratic as she is. Her husband, though, might like it if she did.'

Paul's lips tightened. 'How so?'

Maddie laughed. 'You're better off sticking to the White sisters, or maybe Alice Henderson, if you want the hostess with the mostest. I adore Elizabeth, but she does remind me a bit of my mother! Always wanting things a certain way, people to do as she asks. But she's rather more like those upstart Vanderbilts! The sisters do so much for art and history here. And they do love their dogs!'

'I'll keep that in mind if I want to join the Santa Fe 400, then,' he laughed.

'More like – 200 at the most here. But it can be more evident during Fiesta. You'll see.'

'Come on, you two!' Will called. 'Stop yakking and get to work on that painting, or no gin for you!'

El Delirio, 'The Madness', the White sisters' sprawling estate on the edge of Garcia Street, was already crowded for the pool inauguration when Maddie and Gunther's car rolled to a stop on the graveled drive next to all the other haphazardly parked vehicles. The main house, designed after Laguna Pueblo, was lit up like a beacon, every window sunlight-bright, music and laughter floating out into the warm night. Luckily there was no bitingly chill wind for the swimming pool's big debut.

'The White sisters sure know how to entertain, I'll say that for them,' Gunther said, adjusting his elaborate 'Mayan' costume of white linen pleats and gold lamé, gold sandals on his feet and a towering headdress of red and blue feathers on his head. He'd borrowed every bit of gold jewelry that wasn't already adorning other costumes. 'Do you think I'll be sadly covered in wolfhound hairs by the end of the night?'

'Oh, I'm sure they're tucked up in their kennels under their monogrammed blankets by now,' Maddie said, and waved off toward the special Baumann-built kennel, its doorway hung with prizes and lined with monogrammed silver bowls. The Whites were very, very proud of their dogs. She dug out her own silver compact from her beaded bag to check her Cherries in the Snow lipstick. Her own costume was rather simple compared to Gunther's, an old white linen nightdress Juanita had trimmed with a length of gold lace and added Maddie's grandmother's amethyst beads. Not very 'Mayan', but certainly comfortable. Maddie was thinking of hosting a pajama party next.

Satisfied their disguises wouldn't disgrace them, they tied on gold satin masks, linked arms, and made their way through the turquoise-painted double gates and along the lantern-lined walkways past artists' studios and guest casitas to the two-story main house.

The sisters from Pennsylvania, like Will and Paul, had arrived in Santa Fe on a cross-country journey, and told people they stopped to have their hair dressed in Santa Fe and couldn't bear to leave it again. So they bought several acres tucked behind Canyon Road and set about making an artistic sanctuary. Maddie and Gunther, jostled good-naturedly by others in white linen and unwieldy headdresses, went down the shallow steps to a flagstone patio, with the tennis courts glimpsed through stands of trees. A pineapple-shaped fountain burbled and gurgled, and they crossed under a huge cotton-wood tree drooping over the fading remains of summer flower beds.

The main house, two stories, was all curved adobe walls and wavy glass windows, leading to a long, partially-open, glass-walled portal lined with blue pottery overflowing with red and pink and orange flowers. They burst past the crowd into a tiny foyer, whitewashed walls laid with red and blue Portuguese tiles, a red Navajo run underfoot. A few smaller spaniels lounged on low stools to judge the caliber of guests.

The Whites' ancient, uber-efficient butler, Knut Goxem,

took Maddie's cloak, and gestured for a maid to offer glasses of champagne before they were funneled into the portal.

It was a glorious room indeed, and Maddie always wanted one just like it for herself, One wall was all windows, looking out to the gardens and the pineapple fountain, while the wall behind them was all doors carved with birds and more pineapples, all of them done by William Henderson, interspersed by paintings, scenes of mountains and sunsets and Native Americans, glowing pottery in stands, and a funny map of the estate sketched by Will, of course.

They tumbled into the main drawing room, two stories with a minstrels' gallery high above, the two ceilings outlined by thick vigas painted in blue and red to match the rugs tossed over the polished tile floor. Old tin chandeliers cast shadowed shapes on the rugs, swaying, and antique dark carved Spanish furniture lurked everywhere, chests and sofas and x-backed chairs. On one wall was a monumental scene of a hunting party, and on the other a life-sized portrait of Martha White. Through one door could be glimpsed a billiards room, filled with players.

A phonograph played, 'Baby, Baby Blue Eyes', and couples circled the floor between the furniture. Maddie sipped at champagne and studied them; John and Dolly Sloan, him refusing to be in costume and still in his battered felt hat; the Shusters, Will dancing wildly while Nancy spun in slow circles; Gus and Jane Baumann; the Hendersons; Witter Bynner, who no doubt would insist on telling them a poem later; Fremont Ellis, short, hair brilliantined to a high shine, with his beautiful wife Laurencita. Even Paul Vynne was there, and he waved at her with a half-full whiskey tumbler. They all seemed to be having a grand time.

Maddie turned to examine a new antique of the Whites', a seventeenth-century Spanish cabinet elaborately carved with leaves and vines and blossoming flowers. She wished she could capture movement like that with her paints, that feeling of springtime. El Delirio certainly held enviable treasures, from medieval tapestries to gleaming pottery from local pueblos, Impressionist paintings and French baroque furniture, all perfectly displayed yet made cozy, inviting.

'It's a gorgeous place,' Paul Vynne said, appearing beside Maddie to hand her a fresh champagne. 'I can't believe the breadth of their collection.'

'The Whites do have glorious taste, it's true. See that Renoir over there? And this cabinet, a new acquisition from Seville, I think. Even their garden has all the finest specimens of flowers and trees! They also have a beautiful choice of illuminated manuscripts in their library.'

'Oh, yes, they showed one to me when I wandered past earlier, a beautiful little prayer book. They said it belonged to Catherine of Aragon, but I'm not completely sure.'

Maddie laughed, and nudged at his shoulder. 'You've made friends fast. Going to stick around here a while, then?'

He laughed, too, and it sounded a bit rusty, as if he didn't use that laugh much. 'I wouldn't mind. Your stupendous weather, the sky. The people. I think I could get some great work done here.'

The door to the salon opened, and more partygoers flooded in. Unlike the wild, artistic crowd already spinning around the dance floor, they were couples from old Santa Fe families, along with Dana Johnson, the newspaper editor, and a few wealthy cattlemen in town from their ranchos. Most of them wore their costumes from whatever Fiesta ball they'd just left, which Maddie guessed must have had a Renaissance theme judging from all the fluttering veils, embroidered 'armor', and draped sleeves. But one couple, the last to come inside, wore regular evening clothes, a dark suit and a navy blue satin gown accented with pearl jewelry and a mink-edged shawl. Ricardo and Catalina Montoya.

His spectacles glinted as he coolly surveyed the gathering, as if daring anyone to say anything about the rumored business failings. No one did.

Maddie started to wave at Catalina, but something held her back as she watched them. Catalina fussed with her shawl, glancing away and then back again before she finally touched Ricardo's sleeve and whispered a few words to him. He glanced down at her, shook his head, and she turned away. Alice Henderson came to greet her, the two of them disappearing into the crowd.

'Maddie, my love, shall we dance?' Will called, and Maddie turned to find him rhumba-ing toward her, a rose between his teeth. She couldn't help but laugh, and glanced over at Paul to share a joking glance about their friend's *joie de vivre*. He too had disappeared in the growing, and growing more raucous, crowd.

'Of course,' she said, and gave the empty glass to a maid. She saw Catalina again, talking to Alice and a few other ladies, a strained smile on her pink-painted lips, but Ricardo was nowhere around.

Will spun her into a two-step to the tune of 'Society Swing', nearly bumping into the next couple. 'I think they should move everyone out to the pool soon, or all their guests will be on the floor!' she said, giggling.

'No worries about *that*! You know us – nothing ever flattens us, not even Poquaque Lightning. Which would *never* be served here at El Delirio!'

'How is Zozobra progressing? Is he ready for his big night?'

'It will be splendiferous, my dear! All our glooms gone in a swirl of ash.'

There was the squeal of the phonograph as someone lifted it from 'Society Swing' and put on something else. 'Tell Me, Pretty Maiden', a sweet ballad popular many years before.

'I admit I do love this one, even though it's distinctly unfashionable,' Will said.

'You love all the songs, the sweeter the better,' Maddie answered. As they spun again, slower to the old-fashioned tune, she glimpsed Catalina standing near the phonograph. She looked wistful as she stared down at the record, her large, dark eyes shining with tears. Her husband took her arm, and said something close to her ear, making her shake her head. She said something to him, and anger clouded his face as he gave her arm a shake.

'Will,' Maddie said. 'Do you think something is amiss with Catalina Montoya?'

'Hmm?' he said, his thoughts clearly a hundred miles away, as they so often were, spinning on his art and his parties.

'You know – the Montoyas. She looks a bit upset.'

Will turned them edge-wise in the pressing crowd so they could see Catalina. Ricardo had left her, and she stood alone near the wall, a little frown on her face, her shawl drawn close around her. 'Oh, you know. Probably just – marriage. They've been together an age, haven't they? It happens that way.'

His gaze flickered toward his own wife. Nancy hovered near the bar beneath the gallery's overhang, her satin-slippered toe tapping as she frowned at the crowd.

'But I'm sorry, Maddie love!' he said, and gave her an apologetic little squeeze. 'You weren't married long enough for such things, were you? You've only had the hearts and flowers.'

Maddie sighed as she thought of Pete, her dear sweetheart who died in the mud of France during the war, and the too-short days they had together as husband and wife. Maybe they would have dwindled to quiet arguments at parties, who knew? She would have liked to have found out, but she wanted better for her friends, for Will and Nancy and Catalina. 'Yes. Hearts and flowers.'

'And you'll have them again! Don't you worry about the Montoyas. People like them always smooth out the cracks. Old money and all.'

Maddie still worried about Catalina, the way she'd seemed sad about that song, her husband's lack of solicitude. The way he left her alone. They turned again in the dance, and she saw Catalina was no longer by herself. André Fernandez stood with her, the two of them whispering, and a tiny smile touched Catalina's lips.

'My dear friends!' Elizabeth White called, and everyone turned like a tidal wave to see her standing in the gallery, her elaborate gold and white gown and headdress sparkling. The music ended abruptly as she waved her bracelet-laden arms. 'Thank you for joining us tonight in our ancient Mayan world. We are no longer in our present day, all mad rushing and hurrying! We move back through time as we enter the night. Let our procession begin!'

Maddie felt Gunther grab her hand and tug her into line behind everyone dashing out of the salon and along the windowed gallery into the garden. They giggled like kids as they did indeed step out into the star-dusted night, the pounding of drums leading the way. Footmen in gold and white togas lined the terraced pathways, holding torches to light the stone steps, and lights blinked and flickered in the trees overhead. Maddie wondered what her mother would think of it all, in her dark, grand, staid New York dining room.

'Not much like Manhattan, is it?' she said.

'Thankfully not, darling,' Gunther answered. 'How bored we'd both be there!'

They made their way up a winding, narrow flight of flagstone steps, past studios, the darkened tennis courts, to a large space behind the kennels that had once been an open field leading to an arroyo beyond. This was where the new pool waited, also cold, pale stone, much larger than Maddie'd been expecting, deep and silent and austere in the moonlight.

The tunic-clad torchbearers fanned out around the tiled edge, and their flickering lights cast dancing phantoms over the wine-dark waters. Maddie wished again she held a paintbrush to capture the otherworldly effect, the lights and the subtle colors and the crowd.

Elizabeth and Martha White climbed up on to a gossamer-draped dais built beside the diving board, Witter Bynner behind them, his stout figure swathed in chiffon and linen, a towering gold-beaded headdress making him lean back with its weight. Maddie wished she'd thought of wearing something like that, too.

He brandished a scroll, and read one of his 'poems for the occasion' that made him famous all over Santa Fe. 'But I, his herald, have been told – because his Majesty is suffering from a royal cold, That I may lift my voice this day in a cadenza, And by the gods to lift his influenza!'

As usual, it made little sense, but everyone cheered anyway as he bowed right and left.

'Let this sacred pool receive our homage,' Martha cried, and her sister lowered her arm to signal a flare of torches tossed into the pool. They sizzled and popped, and the drums started banging again as everyone danced away back down the path, toward the champagne fountains set up on the patio.

Maddie soon found herself alone for a moment, there at the edge of the 'sacred' pool. She still heard those drums, the laughter, yet it seemed very far away, muffled by a mist even though the night was clear. She thought of one of the twins' favorite stories, one they begged her over and over to read even though it scared them silly. La Llorona, the spirit of a mother who had drowned her own children and now wandered beside the water, wailing for their return, weeping her grief.

She peered down at the deep water below her feet, and for an instant fancied she saw a person sinking there.

Suddenly, she heard a movement, a footstep along the stone ramp up to the pool, and she blinked into the night sky, that spell still catching at her. She was surprised to see it was Ricardo Montoya. He looked pale in the moonlight, his spectacles gleaming, his expression unreadable.

She glanced past him, but didn't see Catalina. When she looked back to him, he seemed as surprised to see her there as she was to see him. He quickly covered that surprise with a wry smile, and took a silver cigarette case from inside his evening jacket.

'Mrs Alwin?' he said, offering it to her. She shook her head, and he lit one for himself. For an instant, in that flaring glow, he seemed a bit – was it sad? Over whatever he and Catalina quarreled about?

'I just wanted a bit of a quiet moment. I guess we don't have to go to London or New York for romantic stage comedy, do we?' he said. He gestured with his cigarette, taking in the party through the arch of trees, the star-dusted sky.

'Elizabeth does have a sense of the theatrical,' Maddie said carefully. Ricardo made her feel rather uncertain, gauche, and she didn't even know why. He just seemed to see so much behind those glasses.

'As we all do. We all *must*,' he answered, staring down into the water. 'I never did enjoy swimming.'

'I'm not sure the Whites really do, either. A good thing, since we live in a desert.'

He gave a surprised bark of laughter. 'Yes, indeed. You see – the theater of Santa Fe. We must be what we aren't.'

Maddie wondered what he could be hiding, one of the town's

leading citizens. The state of his marriage? His business? It was all very odd. They stood there together in silence for a long moment, the distant music sounding ever more unreal.

'Oh, Maddie! Look who I found, wandering like a lost sheep,' Catalina called out of the shadows below the pool platform.

Maddie peered down, and saw Catalina coming toward them, carefully on the now-dim path, her dark blue gown blending into the shadows. She held on to David's arm, and he smiled as he waved up at Maddie.

'It seems we're both found, Mrs Alwin,' Ricardo said. He tossed his cigarette into the pool, where it hissed out. 'No quiet moments after all. Don't tell Catalina about the smoking, eh?' He gave her a little wink, and she had to laugh. Something told her she shouldn't like Ricardo Montoya, but he seemed like a man of many depths. People were ever complicated, and she had the strange sense he was more complicated than most.

'She disapproves of the habit?' she said.

'Well, we all have to keep a few secrets, don't we, Mrs Alwin?' he said softly, staring down into the water.

'If I was a betting lady, Mr Montoya, I'd guess you had more than a few,' she said quietly.

He gave her a startled glance. 'Your artist's eye?'

Catalina and David reached them up the ramp just then, and they couldn't say anything more. Catalina trembled a bit in her satin gown, her shawl lost somewhere, as she stared down into the pool with her husband.

'It's all really not as I would have expected,' she murmured.

'What did you expect, *querida*?' Ricardo asked her, his tone seeming to say he didn't just mean the pool.

A frown creased Catalina's brow. 'I – well, I don't know, really? Something like the little lap pool we have at home, maybe, only – prettier. This is not pretty at all, is it? So austere.'

Maddie glanced around. No, the pool wasn't pretty. Just a vast plain stone basin, large and stark in the middle of the field. Beyond everything was darkness, the plain sloping down toward the arroyo ditch at the back of the estate. The noise and light from the party seemed further away than ever, as if it was behind an invisible wall, and she and David and the Montoyas were cut off from it all.

She reached out for David's hand, and told herself to stop being such a dumb Dora about it all. It was just a swimming pool, just a party, like ones she went to every week. Yet she couldn't quite shake off that odd, cold feeling. That blurry sense of something spinning off into the sky.

Catalina seemed to feel something like it, too. She stepped to the edge of the water, the toes of her satin shoes on the tiles, until her husband impatiently tugged her back.

'We should go,' he said, brisk and distant, very different from the way he seemed to Maddie only a moment before. 'I must speak to Señor Luhan about some business before we leave, and before everyone is too drunk to see straight.'

'Yes, of course. Good night, Maddie! I'll see you soon, yes, to make more progress on the portrait?' Catalina called as she followed her husband back down the ramp.

'Of course, soon,' Maddie answered. As she watched them vanish into the darkness, Ricardo shook Catalina's arm again, and they seemed to quarrel once more.

'You seem cold, Maddie,' David said, and took off his evening jacket to wrap it around her shoulders. It was warm and cozy, and smelled of his lemony cologne, a faint hint of the strong hospital soap. 'It's a lovely costume, but maybe not *quite* the thing for a chilly autumn night?'

Maddie gave a shaky laugh, and drew the folds of the jacket closer, as if she could block out the eerie feeling lingering over the evening. With David there beside her, she *did* feel steadier, more herself.

'It's just an old nightdress Juanita sparkled up with some lace and ribbon. I should have found a headdress like Witter's, it was quite impressive,' she said, and wrapped her hand tight around his arm. She didn't want him flying up into the sky away from her. 'I wasn't quite sure what would be Mayan. Though since I saw a few people dressed as rococo shepherd-esses and medieval knights, I shouldn't have worried so much.'

'I'm sorry I missed the pool dedication,' he said. 'So much paperwork at the hospital these days.'

'Poor David.' She reached up and smoothed the creases of

his brow with her fingertips, making him laugh. She smiled to hear it, and snuggled against his shoulder. 'Not to worry, there's more of Witter's poetry to be found. And there's plenty of party left.'

They linked arms and hurried back toward the house, the light from the lanterns in the trees speckling David's silver and gold hair, casting shadows over the path.

'Are *you* all right, Maddie?' he said. 'You seem . . .'

'Oh, just a little daydream-y, I think. Autumn evenings will do that, you know.'

'What were you talking about with Ricardo Montoya? His wife is so charming, but he always seems to – I don't know, like something important is happening elsewhere.'

'Yes, exactly. We weren't talking about much at all. He doesn't seem at all a talkative sort.' She stopped and stared out over the tangle of merriment on the terrace. People danced around the pineapple-shaped fountain. 'I just – well, I had a very odd little feeling.'

'How so?' David asked solemnly, and Maddie realized that was just one of the many ways he was the cat's pajamas. He always listened to her, took her seriously.

'I'm not sure. I just had a distant feeling there by the pool, like I'd fallen into another world or something.' She gave herself a shake and smiled up at him. 'But I'm being a silly! We should celebrate.'

He laughed. 'Celebrate Elizabeth White's pool?'

'Yes! And you, and me, and being here together, and our friends, and that sky, and the music . . .' She grabbed his hand and pulled him with her down to the terrace, into the thick of the party. They joined the dance, and she forgot her eerie feelings in the fast steps and twirls, the laughter, the joy of being in David's arms, and the evening seemed to slip by.

Until there was a shrill shriek, cutting into the music.

'No! I won't go. I won't do what you say any more,' a piercing wail went up, floating above the party like a bad godmother at Sleeping Beauty's castle.

Maddie went up on tiptoe to see past the dancers pressed around them. Sofia Montoya, Catalina's daughter, the Fiesta *princesa*, had arrived at the party – and not alone.

She wore a shimmering gown of pearl-colored silk and beaded fringe, very stylish and modern, and very short above her knees. Her gold-streaked hair was bound by a beaded bandeau, and her ungloved hand was wrapped around the arm of a tall, burly, handsome, red-headed man – Jake Silverstein, whose family owned one of the large stores downtown and an import business. He looked flushed with discomfort at finding himself a center of attention, but he stayed close to Sofia, his hand tight over hers.

Catalina reached for her daughter's arm, a desperate expression on her face. '*Niña*, come away, let's go . . .'

'No, Catalina, let her have her say,' Ricardo said tightly, a humorless smile on his lips. 'She's come so far to do so, and in such an interesting gown. Yet I'm sure she must have a reason to be here, we did not raise her to go where she has no invitation. Then again, we have taught her many things, such as duty to family, which she ignores.'

'I *was* invited!' Sofia cried. 'Ask Miss White. And I only want to be engaged to the man I love. This is the 1920s, not the 1820s!'

'Love,' Ricardo scoffed, shaking off his wife as she tried to calm him. 'Stop drinking and go home, Sofia. What would Mr Marulis say if he could see you like this? Causing such an unladylike scene.'

'*You* stop this, Papa! Mr Marulis doesn't care about me any more than I do him. I love Jake,' Sofia argued, as everyone near them glanced away, pretending great interest in their drinks or cigarettes or now-whispered conversations. But really they were all avidly watching the Montoyas as if they were a Fiesta melodrama on a stage.

And Maddie knew the Montoyas weren't people who would appreciate that kind of attention one bit.

'It's true, sir,' Sofia's handsome beau said stoutly, holding tight to her hand. 'I love her very much. I have only the most honorable intentions.'

Ricardo took off his spectacles and rubbed at the bridge of his nose as if he was exhausted by it all. 'Honorable? You two would not know the meaning of the word. I have spent my life devoted to honor, sacrificing for it. And here you both stand . . .' He turned away. 'Take her home, Catalina. I blame you for this, for encouraging our children in ridiculous notions. Let her sleep off this nonsense, and hope she is not cast off the Fiesta court.'

Ricardo smiled, like an actor making an exit, and strode out of the salon. Catalina followed, holding Sofia close with Jake trailing behind them, and slowly the party went back to normal. But Maddie knew this bit of theater wouldn't soon be forgotten.

FIVE
The Night of Zozobra

Zozobra was certainly off to a lively start, Maddie thought as she watched the chaos of Will's back garden. The day grew later, the sun sinking through amethyst and navy-blue to coral and gold and ruby-red, and Zozo waited on his dais for his doom as he balefully glared down at the chaos with his huge glowing green eyes, his giant hands fluttering in the cool breeze. Maddie found herself instinctively avoiding that stare, avoiding his lurking anger, and keeping to the edges of the party. The garden was packed, with kids and dogs running around whooping, everyone dancing as the sun sank in a blaze of pink and coral and purple light.

'Maddie, my darling! Dance with me,' Gunther cried, and Maddie laughed as he grabbed her hand and twirled her in a dizzying circle.

'You'll spill my drink,' she protested.

'We *cannot* have that, of course, too, too dreadful.' He handed her half-full glass to a passing stranger, who happily gulped it down, and then led her into a wild Charleston.

'Well, there's always more where that came from at Will's place,' she agreed, and tossed aside her heeled shoes to dance in the dust, twirling and spinning. She threw back her head and laughed, forgetting all about Zozobra's fury. 'You always know the latest steps, Gunther!'

'This step is the Collegiate, all the way from Chicago. Try it like this! You kick like this on the off-beat . . .' He grabbed Maddie's hand and they kicked and spun and flicked.

Maddie tried to catch her breath, both from the energetic hopping-around and Gunther's infectious energy. Her friend seemed to be in an ecstatically good mood, and it made her happy, too. She sometimes worried about him, his loneliness that he always tried to hide, but there was none of that tonight.

It was as if all their glooms were really about to vanish into the night sky. 'I have to slow down! You're too much for me, my love.'

'What's not to be energetic about now, darling? It's Fiesta, our glooms are about to go *poof*, and all our friends are here.' He took two more drinks from someone passing in the other direction, frothy pink drinks of unknown origin.

'I will certainly drink to that.'

'You must come with me soon to a spiffy new club on Palace Street,' Gunther said, as they dodged around another dancing couple. 'It's absolutely gorgeous! Crystal chandeliers, velvet banquettes, champagne . . .'

'Oh, Gunther. I don't know if I can face a club *there* again,' Maddie said with a shudder to remember what happened once at a 'spiffy' club on Palace. She had almost gotten killed chasing a murderer. She'd avoided most speakeasies since then.

'It isn't like *that* at all, my poppet! Though you won't believe who runs it.'

Maddie found herself curious despite herself. 'Who is it?'

'The sister of those abominable Genet/Bennett siblings! It's too, too fascinating. She's nothing like her family, darling, much like ourselves and our gruesome relatives.'

'Gunther! I thought you said it wasn't like *that* at all now. If she's their sister . . .'

'You just have to meet her, dearest, and see for yourself. She's fascinating. And, if nothing else, the Gin Fizzes and Sidecars are heavenly. She really wants to attract an artistic clientele.'

'And are the waiters as handsome as before? Hopefully they aren't quite as untrustworthy.'

Gunther sighed blissfully. 'Ever so, so! Not as much as Will's new house guest, though.' He waved his drink toward Paul Vynne, who had just joined the party from his guesthouse, his salt-and-pepper hair shimmering in the bonfire glow, just like that Renaissance painting she first thought him.

'He showed me some of his sketches,' Maddie said. 'He's very talented, very original. I wonder if Will might persuade him to stay in Santa Fe a little longer.'

'I'd be happy to help in that endeavor. Our little desert paradise could use a little more interest these days, a little more – originality.'

Maddie studied her friend carefully, his little smile, the glow of his eyes, and she wondered if he had feelings for the newcomer. It made her worry. 'Is Paul – romantically inclined, then, darling?'

He took a deep gulp of his drink. 'Oh, poppet, who can really say? One does get small *inklings* sometimes, but it's all so delicate.'

Maddie nodded. Gunther's romances had been a bit unlucky lately, as hers had been before David came along. She wanted so much for him to find the happiness, the scope to discover his real path, that they had all been seeking when they landed in Santa Fe. Or even if they had always been there, like Sofia Montoya. They all deserved to love who they loved.

'Isn't romance always delicate?' she said. 'Never as straight-forward as in books. Then it seems like the tough part is always *before* a couple gets together, all the adventure and danger. Then it's all smooth sailing, happiness always.'

Gunther squeezed her hand. 'Is all well with you and the dishy doctor, darling?'

'Very well. He's lovely, isn't he? And so kind, so easy to talk to. If only . . .' Her voice trailed away as she thought of the long hours he worked, the shadows under his glorious blue eyes. She reached for another drink.

'You can't let him get away! Wherever would you find someone else like him? Always healing people, always smiling, that yummy British accent . . .'

'He could only be found in those Austen pages.'

'And you don't want your Mama hopping on a train to come matchmake for you. She would be sure to drag some stiff-collared Schuylers or Fricks with her!'

Maddie giggled to imagine her mother, tall, stately, silver-haired, marching down the train platform in Lamy with a gaggle of Fifth Avenue magnates behind her. 'Gosh, no! I'm definitely going to cling tight to David. Have your parents been sending threatening letters to you, then?'

Gunther's lips pursed. 'You know they wouldn't. I'm a

blacker than black sheep, and proud to be so!' A burst of drums and trumpets exploded into the night, the sky dark indigo now, dotted with little diamond-sharp stars. 'Oh, come on, my love! This is the Party of Parties, we have to dance until our shoes are in shreds!'

He took her hand and spun her around with a flick of his feet, until she was giggling madly. 'Can I cut in?' a low, velvet-warm English accent said, and Maddie's heart stuttered pitter-pat. Just like Elizabeth Bennet.

'She is all yours, Dr David,' Gunther said merrily, twirling Maddie into David's arms. As Gunther danced away into the growing crowd, Maddie wrapped her arms around David's shoulders and went up on tiptoe to kiss his cheek. He must have just shaved before he came to the party, for he smelled deliciously of bay rum and lemon, and of that wintry-cool essence that was only him. He felt so solid under her hands, so wonderfully *there*. How could she ever bear it if he was gone, like Pete, someday? They had tonight, this party, this music. This sky.

He gave a surprised laugh, and spun her around until the bonfire blurred and she squealed in dizzy happiness. Maybe that night, that sky, was enough. It was everything.

'That's a grand greeting!' he said. 'What were you and Gunther talking about so intently?'

'Oh, just about getting rid of our glooms tonight. And about Jane Austen! How you remind us of her stories.'

His eyes widened. 'I'm hardly a Darcy. I don't have a Pemberley for you.'

'You're more of a – a Tilney, I think. Kind and funny. Anyway, I'm so spiffing glad you could make it tonight.'

'So am I. I'm sorry I was late, a surgery ran long and then I was a mess and dashed to the boarding house to clean up. But I had to see the results of your and Will's handiwork.'

They spun to face Zozobra, glowing white in the darkness. 'He does look fearsome, doesn't he?' she said. 'But soon all that work will go up in smoke.'

'What glooms are you getting rid of, then, Maddie?'

'It doesn't matter. It will all soon be gone!' She just wished she could be rid of all her friends' troubles as easily. 'Tonight is just for fun.'

'I entirely agree.' David held her even closer, and she closed her eyes, certain that no moment could ever be finer than this, ever be more perfect.

A burst of drums, deep and primitive, as if it came from deep inside the Earth itself, louder and more enthusiastic than strictly in tune, flashed into the night, and Maddie and David faced the dais, arms linked together. Witter Bynner, the local poet and bon vivant, costumed in a black cloak, led a procession of musicians, chasing children clad as red 'glooms'.

'Burn him! Burn him!' The shout went up into the purple-black night sky, eager, full of laughter, touched with just a bit of anxiety. Maddie glanced around at the faces of her friends, barely lit with the few torches planted around the garden, and shivered.

Maddie blinked open her eyes as the rose-gold light of morning pierced her sleep. She groaned and rolled over, finding not her own fluffy bed with its bright quilts and soft sheets but the thin cushions of the old iron chaise on Will's portal. She laughed to realize she must have fallen asleep there after dancing for hours, and rubbed at her mussed, bobbed hair.

The day smelled of the freshness of morning, the flowers growing wild in the garden, the tinge of smoke from Zozobra's death throes. She stretched and sat up as she studied the people around her, slumped on pillows on the portal, sleeping in hammocks. Will was poking through the ashes, a frown creasing his lean face behind his spectacles.

'Will?' she called, finding her shoes before she stepped down off the portal. 'Is something wrong?'

He glanced up, his eyes wide. He gestured to the metal backbone of Zozobra, the pitted dais, which was all that remained of the demon. 'I think Zozo got more than he bargained for last night, Maddie.'

He poked his rake at the smoking ashes again. The slips of paper they all wrote their glooms on were gone, but something else gleamed there, smoke-stained but intact. Something she hadn't seen when they sewed Zozo closed the day before.

A set of false teeth, bright white and still attached to fake gums. A pocket watch, the silver marred by the dark gray ashes. The mangled gold frames of a pair of spectacles. The charred remains of a fine, hand-stitched shoe.

Maddie swallowed hard. 'Those weren't there before.'

'No. Neither was this.' Will used a small spade to hold up something else. A human finger bone.

Outside, it was a beautiful day, as if to make what happened before a mockery. How could the world just go on as normal when *that* just happened? But she had to admit she was a bit glad David had persuaded her to go on a walk along the arroyo behind Garcia Street, not far from her house along with the dogs. The fresh air and sunshine helped clear her head a bit, and being with him meant she wasn't alone. Pansy and Buttercup frolicked along, barking at the birds.

She turned a corner and glanced into a tree to see the twittering, raucous birds, but her shoe slipped in the soft pebbly sand of the arroyo's slope. She caught herself on the rough trunk of the tree – and glimpsed something far below that wasn't meant to be there at all. A pale blur – a shock of dark hair, dirty with the sand.

'No, Maddie, stop!' David shouted, his hand shooting out to hold her back. It was all too late. She'd seen it too clearly by then.

It was the body of a man lying face down in the shallow muddy water at the bottom of the arroyo – or part of a man, anyway. Like a mannequin broken and tossed into a gutter, pale and formless. Face down, one mutilated hand thrown out, legs twisted beneath him.

'We should find a – a tree branch, or something. Pull him out,' she said, even as her numb mind told her it was all much too late.

'Yes,' David said simply, in sync with her as they usually were. He found a stout branch, and scrambled down into the arroyo to carefully, delicately, lever the man out, putting him face up.

Maddie tried to look at the scene as a painting in a gallery, a picture composed of elements, colors, shadows, not real life, real death. Just colors, shapes, choices meant to evoke emotions.

David returned in only a moment, though it felt more like a century to Maddie, shivering alone. He held that thick branch in his hands, and carefully laid it aside to dust off his hands in his handkerchief. It wasn't too effective. He swiped his mud-splattered wrist over his forehead, leaving a smudge behind. His jaw was set in a grim line. 'Poor blighter.'

'Indeed,' Maddie whispered, and that one innocuous word seemed almost ridiculous when she considered what they actually stared at. *Nertz*, her exclamation to Will when they dug through Zozobra's ashes, seemed a little more appropriate a word. Even better would be something her old nanny would have stuck soap in her mouth for, to be sure.

She thought of that night Tomas Anaya was murdered, his bloodied body hauled through La Fonda, and she felt yellow-sick.

That soap would be better than the bile rising up in her throat now. She turned away and closed her eyes, forcing the sickness away.

'Definitely deceased,' David said hoarsely. 'No sign of gunshot. No sign of – anything particularly.'

'So no drowning victim? Someone stumbling drunkenly home from a Fiesta party?' Maddie said, and felt very silly. How could he be stumbling home with half his throat cut and head half off?

'Maddie.' David gently took her by the arms, holding her steady. 'I'll wait here. Can you fetch help? El Delirio isn't far, and I know they have a telephone. Have them send for the police.'

Maddie swallowed hard, and nodded. Having an errand helped her focus, helped her feel calm and gentle, as did looking into David's eyes. 'Yes, of course. But you – I can't leave you like this, David darling, all alone, with – with . . .'

He smiled wryly. 'I've seen worse in the war, I'm afraid, love. I'll be quite well, once I know you're safe away from here.' He glanced around them, at the morning stillness, the pale blue sky and dusty arroyo, his eyes narrowed. 'Whoever did this is long gone.' He kissed her once, quickly, sweetly, and squeezed her arms one more time.

The rising sun gleamed on something in the arroyo, and she gasped. 'Look at that handmade shoe, like in the ashes. Is that possibly Ricardo Montoya? Was he – could he be the one in the fire? And here?'

David was suddenly all doctor. He scrambled down into the arroyo and knelt close to the body, scanning it closely. 'I think you could be right. Yes. But go, Maddie! The sooner we call the police, the sooner we can move this poor soul, whoever he is.'

And then somehow Catalina Montoya would have to be told. Maddie thought of that knock on the door, the telegram, the stark, printed words that Pete was gone, and she felt sick all over again. She took off running, Buttercup and Pansy at her heels, as fast as she possibly could, even as she wished she could just freeze things for Catalina and her children.

Maddie paced from one end of the sitting room to the other, completely unable to sit still for a moment. She tidied a stack of books, plumped an embroidered cushion, poked at the fire smoldering in the tiled grate. She could hear Juanita's pots rattling in the kitchen, the music from a Fiesta procession outside the window, incongruously ordinary after what had happened.

It was almost a relief when there was finally a knock at the front door. *Something* would have to happen now, surely! Time would have to tick forward, and she could think of something besides that poor, mangled body in the arroyo.

Not that it would ever quite go away. She hadn't known Ricardo Montoya well, if it was indeed him, and what she did know she didn't much like. But she did like Catalina very much indeed, and no one deserved such an end. She would surely see it whenever she closed her eyes for nights and nights to come.

She sat down on the closest sofa and hugged one of the cushions close to her as the dogs huddled at her feet. She heard Juanita's steps hurrying toward the front door, the click of it opening, the rush of the cool breeze through the house – and the rumble of a deep, flatly accented voice. A familiar voice.

Maddie sighed. Inspector Sadler. Of course it would be him.
She hadn't seen much of him since the film crew left after
that murder, the director killed on his own movie set. They'd
started to get along a bit better then, but she still didn't quite
trust him.

She rose slowly as he ducked through the low doorway of
her sitting room.

'Inspector Sadler,' she said, rising slowly to her feet. She
smoothed her tweed skirt and her long cardigan, serious,
solemn clothes for a serious morning. 'It's been a while since
we met.' Luckily.

He seemed to agree, frowning fiercely as he swept off his
ever-present bowler hat. 'Wherever you are, Mrs Alwin, there's
some kind of trouble for my police department.'

'Oh, believe me, I wish this trouble were very far away.'
She closed her eyes against the memory of what she had seen.
'Juanita, can you fetch some tea, and maybe some of your
almond cake? If the inspector has time . . .'

Inspector Sadler nodded, and she could see suddenly he
looked rather weary, resigned. Not as bulldog-y as usual. 'I'd
sure be grateful, Mrs Anaya. Mrs Alwin. We've been up since
midnight. First all this Fiesta commotion, drunks, fistfights,
my jail cells full of all these brown boys. Now this. A
chopped-up body, of all things! Right here in the middle of
Santa Fe.'

His constable, Rickie, a young friend of Eddie's who
had nonetheless been with the police now for a few years and
ought to be used to such bluntness from his boss, cringed
and blushed.

Maddie shot him a quick smile. 'Do sit down. I'll certainly
help however I can.'

'I know you and Dr Cole found the, er, remains in the
arroyo,' Inspector Sadler said, after he swallowed a whole
piece of Juanita's fresh almond cake. Crumbs trailed down on
to the blue and red Navajo carpet. 'And those, er, bits in the
firepit at Mr Shuster's place.'

'Yes.'

'And you thought then it might be Mr Montoya? The, eh,
rest of him, that is.'

'I did suspect as much, yes.'

'Why was that? It was all a bit, er, unrecognizable.'

It was true it had looked a bit like chops at Kaune's meat counter, Sadler meant. Maddie swallowed hard and nodded. 'It was his shoes. Um – shoe. One. It was quite fine, hand-stitched, calfskin. Though I suppose those things might have been stolen?' It was a faint hope, but she grasped at it for his wife's sake.

That was soon dashed. Sadler took a battered notebook from his coat pocket and flipped through the closely written pages. 'I doubt it. Someone in the department called on Mrs Montoya earlier. Her husband did not come home last night, and the maid told her his bed was undisturbed this morning.'

So the Montoyas did not sleep in the same room, and she didn't know his movements for hours. Maddie turned this over in her mind, trying to piece together the Montoya family picture. 'Is that a usual thing for him? Staying away from home?'

'She thought he was at a meeting of his *cofradia*, planning for the procession,' Rickie said, unusually bold for the usually quiet, awkward young man. Maybe under Sadler's rather rough tuition he *was* moving forward.

'That would make sense,' Maddie said. She knew there were often special Masses at the cathedral, maybe fasting and extra prayers before a procession. Ricardo Montoya would certainly be there for that. 'But it wasn't so?'

'We spoke to a Mr Fernandez, a friend of the family,' Sadler said, with a scowl at his constable. 'He was at the cathedral last night, says Montoya never showed up. We've sent men out to search, ask around, but the town is in such a to-do, who knows how long that might take.' He helped himself to another slice of cake. 'That sort of thing wouldn't have been tolerated when I was in San Antonio. Dancing and drinking all night, crowds roaming everywhere. Hmph.'

Maddie was rather sure that wasn't what the men of Mr Montoya's *cofradia* would have been doing, but she didn't say so. 'How was Mrs Montoya when your department spoke to her? I do hope her children are there to help her.'

Sadler flipped back in his notebook. 'The daughter was. Miss Sofia Montoya. Just back from the morning's procession. A princess of some sort, I gather.'

'Yes. She would have been escorting La Reina.'

'Not dressed very princess-like, they said.' He read from the notebook. 'White blouse, blue wool skirt, cardigan. Mother still in dressing gown.'

'And the Montoyas' son? Juan-Antonio?' Juan-Antonio – who wanted to be an artist against his father's wishes.

'Not home at all. No doubt he was off sleeping off last night's parties.'

Maddie pictured Catalina sitting there in the early morning light, practically alone, the numbness of sudden grief, and shook her head. 'Poor Catalina. How hard it all is.'

'To be a widow . . .' Juanita murmured, and crossed herself. She knew too well what it was like to lose one's husband in terrible circumstances.

'You know her then, Mrs Alwin?' Sadler said.

'I'm painting her portrait. She's very kind. But she had no one else with her?'

'Servants. The place was crawling with them. Butler, parlor maids, a chauffeur – you'd have thought it was Buckingham Palace, apparently.'

'I suppose in a way it is, for Santa Fe.'

Sadler flipped to another page. 'And you were at this Mr Shuster's place last night? That fire business.'

Maddie took a long sip of her tea. 'Yes, I was. Zozobra, old man gloom, ushering in a new season.'

Sadler scowled again. 'This town. Hoity-toity rich folks at one end, and crazy-as-loons artists on the other.'

'No offense meant, Mrs Alwin,' Rickie quickly said.

'None taken,' she said, giving him a blithe smile. She'd long ago learned to brush right over the inspector and his attitudes. 'I'm sure I have my do-lally moments, but nothing to some of my Vaughn relatives.' And that was the truth. Her great-uncle had thought once he was a palm tree and had to be watered. 'But yes, Inspector, I was at Will Shuster's last night. It did not quite end as any of us would have expected. You think the two are connected?'

He cocked his head to one side, studying her closely. She took another sip of tea and smiled. 'Don't you, Mrs Alwin?'

'It *would* rather strain credulity to think two such bizarre things could happen so close together, even at Fiesta. And Mr Montoya did wear spectacles, and he . . .' She felt a bit ill again, and felt ridiculous for turning into such a delicate-stomached Victorian maiden. 'And he wore some fine rings. I think there were fingers missing on the body in the arroyo, and a bone in the fire.'

Inspector Sadler snorted. 'As well as a few other bits.'

'I – I didn't look at it quite *that* closely.'

'We'll know more once Dr Cole does his sawbones work, sure, but I'd say we've found most of those bits of Mr Montoya.'

'Just not what happened before he ended up in a bonfire *and* an arroyo,' Maddie couldn't resist saying.

'Believe me, Mrs Alwin, I'll get to the culprit. New Mexico is supposed to be civilized now, a state these twelve years or more; Senator Fall wouldn't want this nasty business to linger. It's not like some drunk down on Lower San Francisco Street, or a cattle-rustler out in Mora. Ricardo Montoya was an important man.'

'I'm sure his wife and children think so, too. And his employees.'

Sadler had the grace to flush a bit, and harrumph. 'Er – well, sure. That's the biggest thing. They noted that Mrs Montoya and her daughter didn't seem so emotional about it all, but people are strange.'

'Truer words were never spoken, Inspector. People *are* strange.'

'I saw a widow who tried to eat her dead husband's kidney once,' Rickie said. 'Didn't succeed, though.'

Inspector Sadler gave him a hard glance. 'So, Mrs Alwin. I guess Mr Montoya wasn't at this – bonfire thing.'

'No. It wasn't really his sort of soiree.'

'We've had trouble with that Mr Shuster before. Noise complaints, public drunkenness, and such. So, who *was* there? Anything strange happen? Besides dancing around this burning zombie business.'

'Why, Inspector Sadler! I'm surprised you've heard of zombies. I wouldn't have taken you as a reader of *Herbert West: Reanimator*.'

Inspector Sadler fiddled with his notebook, looking rather abashed. 'I have to see what's popular out there at all times, Mrs Alwin. Loonies take inspiration from all sorts.'

'I would imagine so. No, the Montoyas weren't there. Just the Sloans and a few reporters. The Hendersons, of course, they never miss a party. And Paul Vynne. A friend of Will's from back in Pennsylvania. And artist, too. I could make a list for you.'

'We have men at Shuster's right now, thanks.'

Will would hate that, Maddie thought. Cops swarming over his house and land. 'Well, I didn't notice anything out of the ordinary, really. It was just a party.'

He leaned toward her, his eyes narrowed until their beady pale blueness nearly disappeared. Maddie remembered her old nanny with the soap again, and tried not to squirm. 'Are you sure that's all you noticed, Mrs Alwin? We both know you're not just some dumb society broad, no matter how it might look.'

Maddie refused to give in to intimidation – or be insulted. She'd known the inspector too long for all that now. 'Why, thank you, Inspector, you are kind to think I look "society". But I have told you all I remember. It was rather dark, and – well, it *was* a party. A bit confusing. I'm absolutely certain I would have noticed someone putting stray body parts into Zozobra, though.'

Even Inspector Sadler had the grace to look a bit embarrassed about the whole idea, and Rickie smothered a snicker behind his hand. 'I'm sure you're right about that. It wouldn't happen to be someone's idea of a joke, though, would it?'

'A joke?' Maddie said, shocked.

'An artistic statement or some such thing. You read about things like that back East, or over in Europe.' He made Europe sound like some distant planet. 'Sculptures out of a bidet and such.'

'No one I know here is much of a Surrealist. Or psychotic.'

'Montoya,' Sadler said musingly. 'That's a Spanish name. *European.*'

Maddie almost choked on a laugh at the implication, imagining elegant Catalina or the rather stodgy – while he was alive, anyway – Ricardo Montoya coming up with Dadaist schemes. 'The Montoyas and Gomezes have been in New Mexico for hundreds of years, I think. And I am sure they aren't interested in Dada or Der Blaue Reiter.'

'Whatever that is,' Sadler huffed. 'Sure. Never know about kids these days, though. They don't want to work like we did when I was young. There's this Princess Sofia and her brother, yeah?'

Constable Rickie looked affronted about 'kids these days'.

'I could sketch what I remember of Will's party, and of the . . .' Her laughter faded as she remembered the cold, terrible reality of that morning. 'The scene in the arroyo. If that would help.'

Sadler seemed reluctant, but finally, when Juanita held out another piece of cake, he nodded. 'You were a bit helpful, I guess, Mrs Alwin, on that film set business. You know how to talk to artsy folks like that. I'm no good at that round-about fol-de-rol. A straight-to-the-point man, that's me.'

Maddie could well believe that. But still – Inspector Sadler admitting he wasn't so good at something? She glanced out the window to be sure one of the pigs from the farm up the street wasn't winging past. 'My old nanny used to say you can catch more flies with honey. I didn't understand her back then. Now I do see her point. People like the Montoyas . . .' And like the Vaughns, the Astors, even Pete's sweet Alwin parents . . . 'They aren't used to being questioned, to looking below the surface.'

'Maybe then, Mrs Alwin, you could do me a little favor,' Inspector Sadler said slowly, eyeing that cake.

Now she was *sure* the whole pork farm would soar by. 'Me? Do a favor for *you*?'

'I have to call on Mrs Montoya myself. Would you come along? A lady's presence might be a comfort. Make them talk a bit more free.'

And maybe help shield Catalina from some of the inspector's

rougher edges. Maddie remembered too well how it felt to be a widow. 'I would be happy to be of assistance, Inspector,' she said sweetly. Honey and flies. And Inspector Sadler was such a large fly. 'Anything I can do to help the law.'

SIX

Maddie had never been to the Montoya house, and it wasn't quite what she might have expected. Most of the prosperous older families lived close to the center of town, in adobe casas owned by their forefathers since the 1700s, expanded and added on to over the decades. Ricardo Montoya probably started at the old Montoya compound on De Vargas Street, where Maddie knew his sister lived now with her numerous children and grandchildren.

But Ricardo ended up behind high walls of expensive imported brick and an elaborate wrought-iron gate heading up into the foothills where Santa Fe could be seen spread out below like a patchwork quilt. As Inspector Sadler rang the large bell at the gate, Maddie studied it all with great interest. She was used to isolated grandeur, of course; her grandparents had one of the largest Newport 'cottages' with a grand view of the sea.

But this was different, it felt like it had been dropped on this ground from somewhere else entirely, built to show off something new. Two stories high, painted a mellow pinkish-brown, with a large balcony wrapped around the top story, centered with a courtyard complete with rose-beds and a pool, it rolled down to manicured gardens. It was clear no expense had been spared here.

A manservant, tall and slim, with golden-streaked hair and cheekbones that could cut glass, very well-dressed for garden work in gabardine trousers and an emerald-green silk shirt Gunther would envy, came loping along to unlock the gate. A black crepe band around his upper arm was the only sign of mourning.

'*Sí?*' he said without much interest.

'I'm Inspector Sadler, come to see Mrs Montoya about the

matter of her husband,' the inspector said with his usual pugnacity, flashing his badge.

'And I am Mrs Alwin, Mrs Montoya's friend, here to offer my condolences,' Maddie added in a gentler tone. 'I won't stay long, it must be all upheaval here.'

The man shrugged, all elegant indifference. Maddie was sure Bridget Luther would absolutely love to find him for her next movie. 'Not so you'd notice, really. I'm Diego, by the way. Major-domo here. Also chauffeur.'

He led them up the winding, raked gravel driveway toward the house. Aside from the ominous dark sedan Maddie knew was from the Rivera Funeral Parlor parked at the side, Diego was right – nothing appeared amiss at all. No one was around. A daily sort of day.

A housekeeper waited at the open front door, like a figure from a Dickens novel, stout and neat and silver-haired in a black silk dress, a ring of official-looking keys at her gilt belt.

'A policeman to see Señora Montoya,' Diego announced with an insolent grin that made both the housekeeper and Sadler tsk. 'And this is Señora Alwin.'

The housekeeper's lips pinched tighter, and she gave the keys at her waist a rattle. 'It is not a good time. The poor Señora is exhausted.'

'There's never a good time in a murder inquiry, Mrs . . .' Sadler said, taking his hat in his hand and making a little bow. Maddie was impressed. Maybe he was understanding now about honey.

The woman did look a bit mollified. 'Mrs Hurst.'

'I do need to speak to her as soon as possible, Mrs Hurst, if we are to stop this from happening again. I'm sure you understand. We'll be quick, but we can talk to her here or at the jail. I have a job to do, you know.'

'I do understand about jobs.' Mrs Hurst sighed deeply, and Diego laughed as he sauntered away around the corner of the house, whistling a jazzy tune.

'The insolence,' Mrs Hurst hissed, and Sadler nodded in sympathy. 'Why such a respectable house keeps him on, I shall never know. It will probably be different now. Well, you had best come inside. I have enough work to do without people loitering in the garden.'

Inside, Maddie studied the foyer. It was like something out of an ancient castle, the Escorial maybe, rising up to a rotunda with family portraits lining the dark green-painted walls between swords and shields and banners embroidered with family crests. There was even a suit of armor, tucked under the staircase that swooped upwards with carved, gilded banisters and dark green carpet on the steps. It smelled strongly of the arrangements of lilies and carnations newly delivered from Rivera's and arranged on every marble-topped table.

Maddie noticed one thing out of place, a low rack lined with outdoor shoes, waiting to be cleaned, and she remembered the pebbled, damp soil of the arroyo. She made a note in her mind to examine those boots and stout walking shoes to see who might have been walking there just recently.

'Follow me, then, Inspector,' Mrs Hurst said. 'Mrs Alwin, if you would care to wait in the sitting room. I will have some tea sent in.'

'Thank you, that would be most welcome,' Maddie said. Inspector Sadler tossed her an almost desperate glance as the formidable housekeeper led him up the grand staircase. Maddie just smiled, and waggled her fingertips at him, and turned toward what she supposed to be the sitting room. It was expensively if unfashionably decorated, with heavy, dark wood carved sofas and chairs upholstered in deep red velvets and brocades, a red Persian rug spread on the flagstone floor. Several paintings hung on the white-painted walls, portraits of glowering ancestors, a Murillo Madonna, and something that might almost have been a Velázquez but something looked strange about the clouds. She looked for a signature but couldn't find one.

Through half-open glass doors she glimpsed the courtyard, roses fading in the cooler light but still lovely pinks and yellows. It featured a long, narrow pool for swimming laps, an oddity in water-hungry Santa Fe which Maddie considered a bit strange, considering Ricardo's dislike of the pool at El Delirio. But maybe Juan-Antonio Montoya used it; they all said his parents expected him to attend a fine Eastern university, and

being athletic was a must there. No one swam now. In fact,
there didn't seem to be anyone around at all, not even the
yummy 'major-domo'. The quiet was echoing.

Maddie wondered where Ricardo kept his papers, anything
interesting she could glance through looking for a clue, no
matter how tiny.

'Maddie,' Catalina said, slipping into the sitting room as
silently as a wraith. She looked rather wraith-like as well, pale
and slim in a simple black crepe dress and her pearls, her hair
caught in a low knot at the nape of her neck, her eyes red-
edged but dry. Her expression was one Maddie sometimes saw
on people newly released from the inspector's clutches. The
light 'people person' touch that man certainly did not have.
She had really come to respect him a bit more after the film-
set disaster, but his narrow attitudes wouldn't let him last much
longer in Santa Fe if he kept it up.

'You look a bit pale, Catalina,' Maddie said. She hurried to
take Catalina's thin, black-clad arm and led her to a chaise
set next to the tea table, near the sun from the tall windows.
Catalina gratefully sank down on to the silk cushions, closing
her eyes for a moment as if exhaustion washed over her. They
were lined with purplish shadows, her cheekbones standing
out sharply, her shoulders like bony wings under the loose
folds. of her bodice. The light glimmered on two antique jet
combs set in her hair, her only jewelry those pearls except for
a saint's medal on a thin chain around her neck and the old
gold wedding ring. It glinted as she reached for the teapot.
'When did you last see him?'

'Oh, after that little to-do at the Whites' party, when I
brought Sofia home,' Catalina said. 'He said he had to see
about some business and left. He's often going in and out like
that.'

Maddie tried not to glance at Catalina's shoes, thinking
of the sandy soil, the tiny pebbles, the boots lined up in the
foyer.

'Shall I refresh your cup?' Catalina asked, ever gracious,
and when Maddie nodded she filled the elegant Meissen cups.
She only sipped at her own, though, and didn't touch the cakes
or sandwiches. 'I believe that most persistent inspector has

gone to speak to some of the outdoor servants, so we should have a quiet moment.'

'How are you, Catalina? How are you *really*?' Maddie asked.

'Oh, as well as can be expected, I am sure. My mama always taught us we must stay strong, never reveal our thoughts or feelings.' She glanced at the tray, and suddenly snatched up a lovely little pink iced cake and popped it in her mouth, as if defying her mother's edicts. 'Just as well. If I started wailing now, I'd never stop, and there is so much to do. So much to think about.'

'If there is any way I can help – I remember how it felt when my own husband . . .'

A flicker of a smile, a glimpse of the warm Catalina Maddie had seen in her studio, that shadow of sadness. 'How kind you are. I am hoping to come for a sitting. Next week, perhaps? You will be wanting to finish the portrait, and I would love to escape this house for a few hours. Of course, I will make sure our accountant has paid you for the work in full.'

'Oh, I don't . . .'

'I must! You have worked so hard. And I have to learn so much. Ledger books and stock portfolios! I must find my way quickly, I think.'

'Doesn't Señor Montoya have secretaries and assistants to see to all that for now?'

'Certainly. Mr Lansing is his chief secretary. I haven't heard from him yet, though, and I'm having a rather baffling time making sense of all the things in Ricardo's library. He would never let Mrs Hurst and the maids in to tidy up.'

'Well, I'm sure your children will be a great help, and the rest of your family.' Maddie knew that, like most old Santa Fe families, the Montoyas and Gomezes were extensive.

Catalina gave a strangled little laugh, and reached for another cake. 'My children have their own concerns now. Juan-Antonio was accepted at Harvard for next year, which was Ricardo's great hope for him, and of course we wish for Sofia to marry soon. My husband found her an excellent match. A business acquaintance of his named Marulis. They will be set up for the future.'

Maddie was sure Sofia would have something to say about *that*, after the scene at El Delirio, but she just nodded and sipped at her tea. She'd learned the great value of just listening. 'As for my own family . . .' Catalina stared out the window, her words drifting away as she seemed lost in thought. 'They, too, arranged a fine marriage for me when I was young, and have used Ricardo's connections to help them, but I confess I haven't seen them very much in recent years.' She gestured toward a beautiful arrangement of hothouse lilies and roses in a silver vase, set atop a marble table. The scent was sweet, rich, overpowering as it caught the breeze from the open doors. 'From my brother. He has not yet called in person. Our parents are long dead, and my sisters busy with their grandchildren. Our other brother works on something in oil – something in Alaska. He will not have heard the news yet.'

She rose in one smooth, almost balletic movement and went to look out the doors at the pool and the gardens. Juan-Antonio and Sofia had emerged from the house to lounge next to the water on the metal chaises set around its stone-work edges, whispering together. 'I am rather on my own, I fear. Like you, Maddie.'

'Yes. It can be frightening, true, but also – freeing. Organize things as we like, no one to answer to. I still miss my Pete so very much, but I've found out who I really am here.'

Catalina suddenly smiled, a real, wide, sunny smile. 'I like the sound of that. But I'm not sure where to even begin. Everyone has been telling me what to do since I was in hair-bows.' She sat down again, and reached out to squeeze Maddie's hand. 'Don't mistake me. I have had a good life, a fortunate life. Ricardo was a generous husband, a loving father. As long as we all did as he said, and did it just right. And faithfulness in a husband, as I am sure you had in your Peter, is not – the usual thing.'

Maddie was surprised. She'd heard Ricardo was most faithful to his wife. 'Was he – attentive to you, Catalina?'

'When he had to be. When others were looking at us.' She glanced again at her children, watchful, protective. 'I thought we would live at my parents' house when we married, that he would build a new wing there as my sisters' husbands had.

But Ricardo wanted to come here, build this place. A grand space for parties, he said. But now I do not have to do any of that! Not if *I* do not wish it. That is what you are trying to tell me, Maddie?'

'I suppose I am, yes. You definitely shouldn't have to entertain his friends one jot longer. I shouldn't think you even have to live here any more, if you don't want to.'

'You are right!' Catalina smiled again, and leaned back on her chair cushions. She didn't seem to be overly grief-stricken. Not that Maddie could blame her. She wouldn't be, either, if Ricardo Montoya had been her husband.

Mrs Hurst stepped into the room, as stern as before but with a slightly worried pucker of a frown between her eyes as she studied her employer. 'That inspector says he has a few more questions, ma'am. I told him you were tired . . .'

Catalina waved this away. 'No matter, Mrs Hurst. Better to get it all over with. Shall I come soon for that sitting, Maddie? I won't be able to go to parties for a while, and I suppose Sofia will be glad not to have to attend all her *princesa* duties, but I will want to see friends.'

'Of course, any time you like.'

She impulsively kissed Catalina on her now less-pale cheek, and Catalina smiled back. 'I am glad to have some *real* friends, here, Maddie, truly.'

A young woman in a brown dress and white apron, her dark hair tied tightly back, saw Maddie and smiled. 'Mrs Alwin!' she cried, and gave a quick curtsy under Mrs Hurst's eagle eye. 'My cousin works for you. Juanita Amaya. Well, third cousin of sorts. I'm Priscilla Luhan. She says you're such a wonderful employer. We haven't seen her in ever so long.'

'You must come to tea with her soon, then!' Maddie said. 'Juanita always enjoys seeing a face from home. She'd love to hear how you've been.'

'Oh, thank you, Mrs Alwin!' Priscilla glanced around furtively, and whispered, 'I have some things I need her advice about, see.' She scurried off just as Mrs Hurst came back, making Maddie wonder what she'd seen in the Montoya house.

She continued up the stairs to a long corridor that faced on to the upper-floor balcony. It was lined with several doors, but only a few were open. She peeked into them, taking in a large bedroom that was probably Catalina's, decorated in pink chintzes and silver vases of flowers, and it was clear she slept there alone. A smaller one was next door that might belong to Juan-Antonio, though it was bare of anything personal except one Harvard banner over the narrow bed. No painting supplies or even pictures. The bathroom was quite lavish, with a large bathtub ringed with salts, piles of fluffy towels on a warmer.

The last room before the bathroom was a half-open portal to a library. It had to be Ricardo's, Maddie thought, remembering that no one was allowed to clean in there. The desk was heaped with papers, the wastepaper basket overflowing with torn bits of fine, creamy stationery. She glanced both ways down the hushed hallway, and seeing no one slipped inside to have a glance through those documents. Sadly, she couldn't make much of most of them, they were so thick with legalese, but she made notes of key words to check on later.

A shout and splash from the courtyard brought her back to the present moment, and reminded her she shouldn't be caught snooping. She took one more look at those papers, at the dusty room that already felt thick with absence, and hurried out again.

When Maddie left the Montoya house and parted with Inspector Sadler, the late-morning sunshine was a sharp, clear butter-color, a few fluffy white clouds sliding through a sky varying from turquoise and baby-blue to violet, no sign of rain to spoil the Fiesta food booths a few blocks away. She hurried past dairy wagons making their way with deliveries, artists carrying their pottery for sale to the plaza, workers lugging ladders and buckets of paint.

She paused on the corner where the honey-colored stone towers of the cathedral glowed in the sunlight, sparkling a bit like tiny stars. Jewel-like stained-glass windows shot out rays of ruby, emerald, sapphire. The church building, so elegant and yet so solid, so welcoming, almost tempted her to go inside and see the statue of La Conquistadora (if she hadn't gone off on one of her processions), and maybe to chat with Father Malone.

But she had important errands that day. She cut through the garden between the cathedral and the hospital, a three-story, white-brick Victorian building of solid structure and many windows and walkways. Maddie dashed up the steps and into the foyer. Better to get it over with.

It was an elegant hospital, as such things went, with an Arts and Crafts lunch room, bright murals on the walls, and large conference rooms where there was often music playing. But it was *still* a hospital, all white and clean and efficient, with the familiar smells of disinfectant, the tang of medicine, sudden cries echoing from hidden halls. It made her sad to come there, even though she knew David and his team were the finest in the region and far more patients walked out than did not. It simply took her back to the war, when she volunteered on the wards to keep away grief. No doubt it made David think of the war, of his dressing stations in mud and blood, and of not being there for his wife when she died. Yet he kept on so valiantly with his work.

Nursing sisters rushed past her, crisp and official in their stiffened white wimples and aprons. Several nodded to her, and waved her past as they knew where she was going.

She went to the elevators hidden near the back of the lobby, and when they clanged behind her, she took a deep breath, and shoved her cold hands deeper into her gloves. The more the buttons clicked, taking them lower into the basement, the colder it became.

The elevator doors opened to a bare cement basement, smelling of disinfectant and something sharp and metallic, something like blood and chemicals.

'David?' she called.

'In here,' he said, his voice echoing hollowly. She followed the sound into a small, familiar room, windowless, lined with stainless-steel counters and cabinets with a drain in the middle of the sloping stone floor. A body covered in a white sheet lay on a concrete slab, and she realized it must be Ricardo. He seemed so small now, shrunk from the large, imposing man he once was.

'All right, then, Maddie darling?' David said gently.

Maddie nodded. She didn't want him of all people to know what a bally coward she was! 'Quite! We've been here before, of course.' Though she did wish she'd paid more attention when they found him in that arroyo, instead of just feeling sick.

David picked up a notebook from the counter and flicked through the incomprehensibly written pages. 'It did seem rather odd. A strangling, I thought, at first glance, a brutal fight. Maybe a stabbing.'

'It was none of those?'

'It was – well, Maddie, it was rather odd. He drowned.'

She gasped. 'Drowned? In a dusty field?'

'Not right away. There was a fight.' He folded back a corner of the sheet, and Maddie swallowed past that sick feeling to take a look. 'See this bruised knot on his jaw? Someone gave him a wallop, probably knocked off his glasses, maybe loosened his false teeth, too. He might have been unconscious when he died, but he definitely drowned, and not in *acequeia* water. Clean water, with a bit of some kind of soap or detergent.'

'He wouldn't have had to be fully submerged, would he?' she asked.

'Certainly not. Just the head. It can take less than sixty seconds to drown. Did you notice any tubs or pools nearby on Zozobra night?'

Maddie tapped at her chin, trying to remember that wild night. 'Lots of water tubs. Helen was worried about Zozo catching the house on fire. They have a bathtub, of course, nothing as grand as something in the house of the Montoyas or the Whites. Those families both have pools, too, and the Whites are not terribly far away from the arroyo.'

Maddie shook her head, and did what she did best – visualized a scene. She took a small notebook from her handbag and sketched the scene in the arroyo as she remembered it. She closed her eyes, and then cried, 'When I first saw the scene, I didn't really notice details. I was – well, a teeny bit distracted. But then I realized something, David. Do you see what we *don't* see?'

He studied the scene, his blue eyes narrowed. 'No drag marks!'

'Exactly! It rained a bit the night before, and even though the ground was mostly dry it was still damp. It would have held the marks.'

'So he died there, he wasn't dragged there. Or maybe he was carried. Those foot marks *are* rather deep.' Two sets on the slope, then – one, very deep. 'I don't understand why Ricardo Montoya would be there on the first day of Fiesta, though. He would have been very busy preparing for the procession.'

'Meeting someone, surely. But who? And why there? Is it often a dumping off place for such things?'

'When Manny Delgado killed his brother-in-law last year, he dumped him near there, but no, not usually. It's too close to Garcia Street and Canyon Road; when someone is careful they have the whole mountains as their dumping grounds. Why put them where they'll be found, unless . . .'

'That's what they want? For him to be found?'

'Hmmm.' Maddie studied the battered, purple face of what had once been Ricardo Montoya, and felt such twisting pity. 'But why would he have wandered off anywhere during Fiesta? It was a very important time to him, he had much to do. It must have been very urgent indeed to call him away.'

She thought of the arroyo at night, how dark and dusty and lonely it seemed, with only the shrill of a coyote in the background. She seldom walked the dogs there, and the girls were forbidden.

'He was surely meeting someone,' she said. But who and why?

'There were bits of stationery found in the pocket of his pants, finely made but ripped to pieces, perhaps it was a note to or from someone. And the bit of water at the bottom of the ditch was very cold,' David said. 'Maybe someone tried to preserve the body, confuse the time of death. Then when he dumped it, something scared him, he ran off and meant to finish the job later.'

'Or maybe to leave a message? Was there anything on the body, or in the clothes?'

'Just the usual. Robbery not a motive. The watch was left with the body, there was money in his pocket, and the wedding ring and family signet on his fingers. Only those flakes of stationery in the pocket, water-logged and ripped into shreds. And these rather odd little hairs caught on his coat. Miss Thomson upstairs is quite good at cryptanalysis, she'll take a look at the papers for us. Other than that, nothing.'

'And his shoes?'

David picked up one of Ricardo's lace-ons. 'Finely made. Italian, I'd say. Exquisite leather, well-maintained. Sand caught in the treads, of course, and water stains, but who can tell from where. The other is missing. Maybe in Zozobra?'

Maddie thought of all the shoes in the Montoyas' foyer, all the shoes in town. 'Who had it in for Ricardo Montoya? He was a pillar of the town!'

David laughed humorlessly. 'Too many, it seems. Come, have lunch with me in the lunch room, tell me what you found at the Montoya house.'

When Maddie stepped out of the gates of the hospital garden and made her way along the walkway toward the plaza, it felt like a whole different planet from the white, cool, anti-septic silence of the hospital. It was all color and heat and noise, children running shrieking down the street between the narrow adobe shops, the wooden walkways lined with blue-painted portals, dust clouds shimmering and dissolving the sunny air. The breeze carried the smells of the bouquets of flowers girls in embroidered skirts sold from baskets, the rich scents of food from the plaza booths. Lamb on sticks, candied apples, popcorn, candy corn, tamales, *tres leches* cakes . . .

A brilliantly colored carousel, the famous Tio Vivo, made its trip round and round in the middle of the plaza under its yellow and white striped awning, brightly painted horses and wagons and giraffes. Maddie glanced at Pearl and Ruby seated in one of the carriages, attended by Eddie, and she waved at them merrily despite her dark doubts.

A mariachi band played on the bandstand, a lively dance that had couples on the cleared space before the stand spinning and stamping and laughing. The red and green and turquoise ribbon trim of the girls' skirts, the silver embroidery of the musicians' pants and the feathers of their large hats fluttered and sparkled, banishing any darkness from the party.

Maddie bought a candy apple, despite hearing Juanita's voice in her head that she would certainly ruin her teeth, and wandered the plaza, just watching the people and the merriment and the wonderful day. A puppet theater put on a tale of a coyote dressed as a grandma in long white nightgown in order to hide out from the hunters, just like Little Red Riding Hood, with a Santa Fe twist. The puppets were created by Maddie's friend Gus Baumann, who had modeled Zozobra's head (and then remade it over and over when it was too small!), and they were exquisite and beautifully detailed, their joints moving just like a human's would. The children shrieked at the coyote-granny's exploits.

In the distance, Maddie glimpsed Will's bright red hair as he led a conga line along the edge of the plaza, everyone singing. Two elderly couples carefully stood up from the green-painted benches and waltzed as elegantly as they must have in their youth. How could she ever leave such a place, ever live anywhere else? Yet how could she keep her little paradise safe from chopped-up bodies in arroyos?

She hurried after Will when he peeled away from the dancers, calling his name. He glanced back, his expression distracted before he smiled. 'Maddie! How are you? What a dreadful time, eh? Who would use my Zozo for something like – that?'

'Truly gruesome.' She reached out and squeezed his hand. 'How are you?'

'Keeping busy. Fiesta must go on!' He held up a brown-paper-wrapped parcel. 'I'm just headed to the museum to drop this off. The Cinco Pintores are hosting another exhibition this winter, hoping to make a wee splash. Walk with me?'

'Of course.' She linked her arm in his and they turned into the crowd on the plaza, toward the thick, square towers of the museum. 'Busy, yes?'

'Oh, certainly, certainly. But poor Helen – she can barely sleep for thinking about it all! I'm sure what happened was a moment's mania, a passing lunatic or something, not someone set on serial chopping-up. She just isn't so sure. She reads so many detective novels.'

She wasn't the only one, Maddie thought, remembering all the books piled on her nightstand. 'How terrible for her.' It would certainly be better to imagine it was what Will said, a passing lunatic or something, yet she wondered if Helen Shuster didn't have the right idea after all. How would a stranger know about Zozobra? Yet how could one of the partygoers that night have left the grim remainders without anyone noticing? And what was Ricardo doing near there at all? 'Have the police been to see you?'

'Oh yes, yes. That Sadler! I have a mind to dress up as the man for a costume party one of these days. It would be so easy. A fake mustache, a bowler hat . . .'

'Like the time you pretended to be Olaf the Swede?'

'Well, Sadler's accent might be a bit different from dear Olaf's, yes! But I did talk to him today. I couldn't be of much help, of course. I was so busy with the party, making sure there was enough hooch, that nothing caught on fire and no one was sick in my vegetable patch again. Helen was so angry that time her zucchinis were ruined! I didn't see anyone looking suspicious.'

'No one was lingering around Zozo before the fire?'

'Not that I saw. Once we closed up the glooms and before the fire itself, I never saw anyone go close. We made him look too fearsome!'

'Then it must have been done before the party. That day, maybe?' Maddie wondered exactly what Ricardo Montoya did the day of his death. Catalina said she hadn't seen him after the El Delirio pool bash.

'I suppose it must have. Surely, though, I would have noticed someone dumping a severed finger.'

'Were you there watching all day before?'

'Well – no.' Will frowned as he considered. 'I had to make a run for more booze, and Helen took the kids to see Tio Vivo. We'd done most of what we could to get ready for the party by then. But anyone could come into the garden if they knew what they were looking for.'

'So you noticed nothing at all strange the last time you examined Zozo?'

'Nothing at all. Whoever did it closed Zozobra up tight after.' He stomped his feet hard into the pavement, cursing. 'I don't understand why Ricardo Montoya was anywhere near my house to even be stuffed into Zozo! He isn't – wasn't– the sort to hang about with all us wild bohemians.'

'No, he wasn't.' Unless one of those 'wild bohemians' had invested with him and been singed, as a lot of the town seemed to have been. She thought of his strange demeanor at El Delirio. 'But he didn't need to be there, really. Whoever killed him could have just known about Zozo and took the – the bits there with him, put them inside while you were gone.' She felt suddenly queasy at the thought.

'Maddie, love? Are you quite all right? You looked a bit grayish there.'

'Yes, just a little sick-making.' She sucked in a deep breath, smelling the candy apples and popcorn of the Fiesta booths, a hint of piñon smoke from someone's fireplace.

'Of course, it's all so disgusting. We're all sick from it. How could something like this come into our little town? It's the kind of thing we're all running from back East!' They'd reached the shallow front steps of the museum, and Will squeezed her hand. 'Why don't you come inside for a while? Look at some paintings. That always steadies me.'

Maddie laughed. To Will, painting was the panacea for anything, and usually she would completely agree with him. Not today, though. Today she just wanted to feel the sun on her face, hear laughter, be around people for a while. 'Later, Will darling. I can't wait to hear all about your new exhibit. I might head over and see how Helen is doing.'

'Good idea, she'd love that. And come to dinner as soon as this Fiesta madness is over!'

Maddie nodded, and turned back toward the plaza.

SEVEN

'Why won't Pansy keep her hat on, Miss Maddie?' Pearl cried, stomping one patent-leather Mary Jane shoe as the dog tossed her ruffled bonnet to the ground again, and Buttercup proceeded to chomp it.

'She's ruining the parade!' Ruby wailed.

Maddie bit her lip to keep from laughing at the twins' Drama. 'My darlings, I'm sure Buttercup and Pansy will be complete angels, compared to most of the pets at the parade. Remember Andy Dormer's donkey? It grabbed a whole pig from the butcher's window and ran all across the plaza with it. No one knew the creature could move so fast.'

Juanita laughed as she sewed up the ribbons of the canine bonnets, making sure they fit closely. '*Dios mío*, that was a sight! And then the Lujans' collie snatched it from the donkey. These dogs would never do such a thing.'

'So true. They're much too small to reach the window,' Maddie said as she painted the last touches on their sign and attached it to the little green wagon Eddie brought from work. *Las princesas de Casa Madeline.* Gunther had added some little purple flowers, sacrificed from one of his beloved cravats, and Juanita had sewn up garlands and wreaths from some old tinsel. Maddie thought it all looked rather spiffy.

Despite all the uncertainty, and the strong possibility of donkey disaster at every corner, the Desfile de los Niños was her favorite event of Fiesta. One of Will's new concepts for his Pasatiempo, not part of the traditional Fiesta, it was hugely popular. No politics, just adorable kids. Most of the town's children insisted on dressing up their pets – dogs, cats, llamas, guinea pigs, even chickens sometimes – and making them parade through the streets in floats and tableaux. The creativity was amazing; spectators never knew what was around the next corner.

'Pansy! No!' Pearl shouted, as Pansy once again made a break for it, her lacy bonnet askew. She obviously didn't want to be a fairy-tale princess. Buttercup just sat down on her cushion in the wagon, her brown eyes full of resignation.

'We'll never win first prize,' Ruby murmured. 'Melanie Parker from school said her cats are going to be Red Riding Hood and the Wolf!'

'That doesn't sound like it will work out very well. And Pansy and Buttercup are far superior to any cats,' Maddie reassured them. She and Juanita fastened the dogs down on their cushions, and smoothed out their lacy Elizabethan collars that matched the trim on the girls' new pink and pale green velvet dresses and little hennins. 'And you two look absolutely gorgeous! Like something in that film we saw last year!'

'*When Knighthood Was in Flower*,' Juanita said with a little sigh. She had loved Forest Stanley in that one.

'Yoo-hoo! Don't you dare leave without me,' Gunther cried, hurrying over from between their garden gates, purple ribbon streamers over his arm. More lost cravats. 'You need these to flutter in the breeze behind you! All right, nearly showtime, my dears. Are we ready? How are my leading ladies faring?'

'Buttercup and Pansy are terrible divas, Gunther. Bridget Luther was nothing to them, I'm afraid. But Pearl and Ruby are perfect!'

'If Pansy would only cooperate,' Pearl grumbled.

'No fear, my most gorgeous *princesas*, we shall have a great success today!' Gunther made sure the wreaths were straight, that the two towers at the end of the wagon, painted by Maddie to look like stone, were steady, and attached the streamers. Buttercup and Pansy did indeed start to fuss and snarl a bit, but a few stern words from their adored Uncle Gunther, who often snuck them bits of bacon, soon had them perfectly still.

'Gunther, you *are* a miracle-worker,' Maddie said. She reached for her drawing pencil to add one more flourish to the sign.

'They are just like us – they want to be stars! I told them no wild pack of mutts could ever win first prize. Now, let me just fix Buttercup's lace here . . .'

The twins dashed back into the house to fetch their own cloaks, their mother hurrying behind them to adjust their hems, and Gunther leaned closer to quickly whisper, 'What did you learn yesterday, Maddie? Something that made it worthwhile to spend time with the gruesome inspector?'

'Quite. I went with him to the Montoya house. Poor Catalina!' She lowered her voice and whispered, 'Then David went over the autopsy with me. You'll never guess!'

'Strangled? Shot? Stabbed?'

'Drowned! We did find him – what there was left of him – face down in that arroyo. But he didn't drown *there*. Soap was in his lungs.'

Gunther's eyes widened. 'So he was dismembered and taken to the arroyo? Shocking! But why? What a great deal of trouble. Where did he come from, then?'

'That is exactly what we have to find out.' Maddie took a deep, frustrated breath. 'Oh, Gunther, how can we fit these tiny, strange pieces together at all?'

'We must call everyone together for a consultation soon, once we can gather a few more teensy clues,' Gunther said. 'You, me, Juanita, Dr David, Eddie, maybe Father Malone?'

Maddie nodded. 'See what we each can remember.' Her little 'detection posse' had been very helpful indeed after the film-set murder. They just had to look at this from all different angles, winkle out secrets and tiny, hidden, shiny things.

There was no time to pull it all together now, though. Pearl and Ruby came rushing from the house, their ribbons and velvets and laces gleaming. Unless they were wearing their school uniforms now, they insisted on wearing mismatching dresses and skirts after a lifetime of twin-clothes. Juanita did grumble about how much more time it took to cut out two patterns, buy two smaller lengths of different cloth, but even she had to admit the girls were growing up and needed to find their own style. They both looked so lovely Maddie and Juanita teared up a bit. Even Gunther sniffled.

'Juanita, you have outdone yourself!' Maddie said. She took the girls' hands and twirled them around, making them giggle. 'These are true medieval princesses.'

'Marion Davies has nothing on them,' Gunther said,

applauding as the girls curtsied. 'You should go to New York and open your own couturier shop, Señora Anaya! Your great talents are quite wasted here.'

Juanita scoffed, but a pleased pink flush touched her cheeks. 'Ah, Señor Gunther, you are such a silly! What would I do in New York? No mountains, no large sky, just concrete. I get along well enough here.'

'You should at least try some gowns for the ladies at Catalina Montoya's *sociedad*,' Gunther said, helping the twins into the wagon next to a now-complacent Buttercup and very uncertain Pansy. 'They're having dances and card parties all the time, and I know their frocks are a great source of rivalry.'

'Those *bien damas!*' Juanita said, still pretending to scoff. 'Their dresses are sent from Paris, or at least from Señora Lucille's across from the DeVargas Hotel. They wouldn't hire some old Puebla like me.'

'I bet Catalina Montoya would. Then *everyone* would want to hire you, which wouldn't work out at all well for me, so you shouldn't do it,' Maddie said. 'By the way, I did meet someone who says she knows you, Juanita. Priscilla Luhan, she works as parlor maid for the Montoyas now? She'd love to see you again sometime.'

'Priscilla? Yes, but I haven't seen her since she was a girl!' Juanita frowned in thought, almost crafty. 'I should visit her, take some of my biscochitos. Maybe she's seen something in that house she'd confide in me?'

'Now you're becoming a real detective!' Maddie laughed.

There was no time to talk more. A faint blast of drums and horns, the first practice bleating notes of the band from St Michael's School, reminded them that time was short. They'd end up at the very tail end of the procession if they didn't hurry.

The twins squealed and exclaimed as they spread their skirts around them and wrapped their arms around the dogs, all of them a great tangle of ribbons and laces and streamers. So adorable, so perfectly fairy-tale – if the *princesas* would stop bickering and Pansy stop growling low in her doggie throat.

With Maddie and Gunther pulling the wagon, and Juanita walking alongside to keep order, they made their way through the crowded streets to the assembly area behind the cathedral. Pets in costumes of all sorts were barking and bleating, refusing to get properly in line, as a 'Secret Garden' theme float threatened to run away, and a donkey kicked at his owner. Even Pansy and Buttercup were angels in comparison.

At last the starting trumpet sounded, and the procession made its wobbly, crooked way through the streets, with De Vargas in his armor and the Queen in her fur-edged velvet cloak and sparkling crown leading the way, far ahead of the inevitable droppings the contestants would leave. Maddie glimpsed Sofia in her white satin *princesa* gown, carrying the queen's train, but no Jake Silverstein in evidence.

The twins played their parts brilliantly, after all the movies they'd seen and the *Silver Screen* magazines they'd pored over. They sat up straight, showing off their gowns and veils, smiling, waving, making the dogs wave, too. Once in a while they would toss out a handful of confetti, shimmering in the bright sunlight. They passed the long portal of Casa Sena, its upper-story balconies packed with watchers, and went around the Palace of the Governors and the art museum, the drums and trumpets blasting away, drowning out barks and snarls.

The crowds grew thicker as they approached and circled the plaza. Hanging over the portal of the palace were the Fiesta families' crests. Those crests had hung there for so long, lovingly repainted every year for this week in reds and blues and golds. One of them was the Montoya arms, poplar leaves on a blue shield surmounted by a silver helmet. Would Sofia Montoya have a place there if she married? And how far would she really go to marry the man she wanted?

Maddie went up on tiptoe to study the royal court up ahead. There was no Jake Silverstein anywhere, but maybe he watched from one of the upper-floor windows or roofs that were packed with spectators.

The older couple waltzing though the plaza smiled into each other's eyes, and Maddie wondered if one day that might even be her and David. A soft breeze fluttered through the autumn leaves of the trees, the air smelled of chile, candied apples, and popcorn from the food booths. Despite all that had happened, it seemed an idyllic day.

The parade circled the bandstand and came to a halt. Maddie and Gunther helped the twins from their castle-wagon, and they joined Juanita beside the bandstand to hear the mayor give out the prizes. To Maddie's not-surprise-at-all, Pearl, Ruby, Buttercup, and Pansy won the blue ribbon for originality.

Maddie glimpsed Will and Helen, along with Paul Vynne, nearby, and they waved and clapped for the girls, too, as dancers crowded on to the green.

'Such a great victory for some fizz, don't you think, Mads darling?' Gunther said amid the loud cheers.

'Not for *princesas*,' Juanita said firmly, ignoring her daughters' wheedling to stay 'just a little longer, one more minute!' 'Baths and dinner, then maybe a quick curtsy at the party tonight. *If* I see tiptop manners.'

They marched off, Buttercup and Pansy trailing behind them as they quarreled over a bone one of them found on the ground. A person could barely walk on the plaza now, there were so many people in their bright skirts and ribbon shirts, twirling and dipping and laughing.

'Well, my dear, I doubt there is a Gin Fizz to be found here at all, but I do see a peach juice stand over there!' Maddie said. 'That's a treat we won't see much of now winter is approaching.

'Your wish is my command, darling. Don't move, or I shall never find you again!'

As Maddie took a sip of the sweet, sticky juice Gunther procured, she glimpsed someone through the crowd. 'Gunther, look! That man over there in the striped jersey.'

Gunther followed her gaze, and his eyes widened again. He patted at his carefully pomaded hair. 'My heavens, but you do know how to spot them.'

'Only because we've met him before. He's Diego, the, er, major-domo at the Montoya house.' Maddie told him about Diego and Mrs Hurst, and how they seemed to know more than they were saying.

'He clearly wasn't hired for his – organizational skills, don't you think? He's a looker.'

'Have you ever met him?' Maddie asked.

'Not *met*, though I have seen him once or twice at the Golden Rooster. He's gorgeous, but not really my type,' Gunther said. 'I'm looking to settle down now, and it's clear he's not that sort. He does always seem to have money to flash about. How long has he been at the Montoya house? Do you know what exactly he does there?'

Maddie shrugged. 'I couldn't really say. I did meet Priscilla, a cousin of Juanita's. I think Juanita would want to go visit her, ask around backstage so to speak.'

Gunther watched Diego thoughtfully as the man made his way through the crowded plaza, dancing with a few of the girls, his handsome head tossed back in laughter. 'Could this Diego be friends with young Juan-Antonio Montoya?'

Maddie wondered – *could* Juan-Antonio prefer men, and was that another point of argument with his father? He really only seemed interested in art, but she wasn't sure. 'I don't know. But surely if that was the case, Papa Ricardo would have tossed Diego out *tout suite*. Nothing must mar the golden Harvard boy.' She took another sip of her juice and mulled it all over.

'And they do say Ricardo was a notoriously loyal husband, no mistresses, maybe just one little office stenographer years ago. He doesn't sound the sort who would tolerate any sort of hanky-panky under his roof.'

'But he and Catalina didn't share a bedroom.'

'Hmm. A monkly celibate?'

Maddie laughed to think of the robust, handsome Ricardo as 'monkly'. But then, one never knew about people, deep down. They watched as Diego vanished into the crowd.

'Well, time for my wee little siesta, Mads,' Gunther said. 'Shall we go to that new speakeasy tonight? See if anyone knows our major-domo, or has heard of any sort of Montoya hijinks lately?'

Maddie wasn't really terribly eager to see any Genet-run nightclubs again, but Gunther was right that the best gossip could always be found over a nice Orange Blossom. She nodded. 'Sure. About ten?'

'Sounds spiffing. Should I walk you home, darling?'

'I think I'll explore just a bit more. Maybe see if I can pull David out of his hospital cave for a few minutes.'

'Good luck, my dearest! That sweetie of yours works more than anyone I've ever seen.'

'Except for you, Gunther. Don't think I don't see your light on and hear your typewriter clacking at all hours!'

'Deadlines, darling! Always deadlines.'

Maddie waved Gunther off, and turned back toward the hospital tucked off the plaza next to the cathedral, but she didn't go there just yet. She made her way back toward Camino Monte Sol and the Shuster house.

It was quiet there today, Will and all the other artists at the parade. The row of widely spaced houses where the Cinco Pintores all lived, 'Five Little Nuts in Five Mud Huts', as they said, were empty. She peeped into one of the windows, and didn't see Helen or the kids. Even Teddy the dog was quiet.

Just past the main house, on the low rise of a hill, was a guest casita, where Paul Vynne was staying. The door was propped open on the narrow portal, but no sound emerged.

'Hello?' she called anyway, carefully stepping one foot inside. She couldn't see anything until she slipped off her tinted glasses. The guesthouse was small, just two rooms and a little terrace at the back, and Paul hadn't been there very long, but it looked very lived-in indeed. The narrow bed was unmade, blankets heaped up, and clothes and shoes scattered around. She glanced at them, and noticed sand on the soles of a pair of old boots, splashes of mud and paint on a jacket. The desk beside the bed was piled with books, poetry and art history. There were a few photos propped around them, an older lady in a wide-brimmed hat, a younger Paul with a few schoolboy-looking friends, Will and Helen.

An easel was set up near the back window, a fresh canvas, newly primed, propped up on it. Sketches were strung along a clothesline, and as Maddie examined them she recognized they must be ideas for his railroad work. Scenes of mountains and oceans and exotic flowers, meant to lure travelers onwards. They were very good, skilled and evocative, but somehow missing the emotion and movement she'd noticed in the sketches he showed her before.

She also noticed that his sloppy housekeeping didn't extend to his tools. His brushes were mostly washed, damp and standing upright to dry, except for a few that were still crusted with paint on the side of a basin. They were expensive and well-kept, and she quite envied a fine boar's bristle brush. His paints were from a supplier in New York. Very nice indeed.

Maddie hurried back outside, blinded all over again by the glare of the late afternoon sun. She put on her glasses, and saw Helen Shuster, dumping out a wash-pan toward the remains of Zozobra. She waved at Maddie and called, 'Looking for our messy house-guest?'

Maddie laughed. 'Not at all! I was just looking in on you. Will said you weren't sleeping well, and who could blame you? It's all so gruesome. Your guest *is* a bit, er, lackadaisical in his housekeeping, though, isn't he?'

Helen gave a wry laugh. 'Oh, I'm used to it by now. Artists aren't the tidiest bunch, present company excepted I'm sure. And they're always in and out at all hours.'

'Is Paul a night owl?'

'Probably. Aren't they all? Dashing off to paint moonlight or something. He's quieter than most, which isn't such a bad thing. He's all right. Just a bit of a mystery. Come inside for a drink?'

Maddie was exhausted by the time she strolled through her own garden gate. Canyon Road was far from the merriment of the plaza; all she could hear now was the dull, muted echo of laughter and music.

Juanita and Gunther sat under the portal, lazily chatting over a pitcher of lemonade and some of Juanita's almond cakes, the dogs snoring under their chairs, and Maddie had never welcomed anything as she did the sight of her friends at her home.

'Lemonade, Señora Maddie?' Juanita asked. 'I just got back from seeing Priscilla.'

'Bless you,' Maddie sighed as she collapsed on to a wicker settee beside them and kicked her shoes off her aching feet. As Juanita handed her a cool cut-crystal glass, Maddie examined her garden. 'Have the princesses retired?'

'They were tired out after the parade, but they fussed and

cried about how they are Certainly Not Tired for the longest time. Then Señor Gunther read to them, and they went right to sleep like little angels. May it last,' Juanita said.

Gunther sighed. 'Such is the sadly soporific quality of my reading. It's been deliciously quiet here, though. You've been gone an age, Mads.'

Maddie took another long, fortifying drink of lemonade and told them about her visit to Will's house. 'I was so sure there couldn't be *that* many bathtubs in Santa Fe, but there seem to be oodles! Not to mention washtubs, swimming pools, cisterns . . .'

'I saw at least three bathrooms at the Montoya house,' Juanita said, seeming rather scandalized at such decadence. '*Three!* Plus that pool.'

'The Montoya house?' Maddie asked.

'Oh, I called after we returned from the parade to visit Priscilla! While Señor Gunther watched the twins for me. She told me all about her work there.'

'Did she say anything we need to know?' Maddie asked.

'Well, she didn't seem exactly overcome with sorrow at losing her employer. Nor was anyone else I met in the kitchen. They're paid well, and they all like Señora Montoya, but they say it's hard work.' Juanita leaned closer and whispered, 'Priscilla told me that she hopes to work for Sofia Montoya when she marries and goes to help run her husband's lovely store.'

Maddie and Gunther stared at her avidly. 'So she's really going to marry Jake Silverstein?'

'Priscilla seems to think so. It seems there were quarrels about it all in the last few days, very noisy.' Juanita shook her head at such a breakdown of domestic decorum. 'As I was leaving, I saw a young man coming in – Diego, I think they said was his name. He looked like someone on that film set!'

'Tall, blond-ish streaked hair, heavenly eyes?' Gunther asked.

Juanita nodded. 'That sounds like him. The housekeeper said he was the major-domo, whatever that is. She said Ricardo Montoya hired him, and he never seems to do any work. Señor Ricardo was usually very strict with staff, but not with this

Diego. Priscilla said she's even seen him take things out of drawers and off tables, and he never gets into trouble!'

Maddie turned this over in her mind and finished the last of her lemonade. 'Gunther, you said Diego has money to flash about when you've seen him. Could it be from blackmail as well as theft? Maybe he knew something about Ricardo.'

'Possibly,' Gunther mused. 'That would certainly make sense. What was it, though?'

'They might know more at the speakeasy. We can ask around when everyone is loosy-goosy on Poquaque Lightning. Diego might even be there himself! He looks like he enjoys an expensive drinkie.'

'Good idea, Mads darling,' Gunther agreed.

As Maddie looked out at her peaceful garden, she realized the last place she wanted to be was a smoky nightclub. But surely there *were* lots of answers to be found in those shadowy corners. *Where* did Ricardo drown, how did bits of him end up in Zozobra and the rest of him carried to the arroyo? Would Sofia really marry her Mr now that her father didn't stand in her way? Would Juan-Antonio forsake Harvard? Would Catalina become the merry widow of Santa Fe? What else did people have against Ricardo Montoya?

She shook her poor, confused head, and reached for another almond cake. 'Well, maybe I could at least persuade David to go with us tonight. I should get a dance for my troubles . . .'

EIGHT

'*She shrieked from her soul, "Mis niños!" before the river water filled her lungs. It is said this weeping woman, La Llorona, has returned from the hereafter, searching for her children to claim as her own for all eternity . . .*' Maddie read with a low howl.

'But – she's not *real*, is she, Miss Maddie?' Ruby whispered in a quivery voice.

'Of course she's not real,' Pearl said scornfully, but her eyes flickered doubtfully to the book in Maddie's hand.

'I know that!' Ruby protested. 'I'm not a baby. But there was Melanie at school – she said she saw something walking by the river last week. At night! Crying.'

Maddie firmly shut the book. 'Real or not, my dears, it's never a good idea to go wandering around in arroyos. It's not safe, with all the flash floods from the mountains . . .' And bodies left there. She was horrified to imagine the girls coming across such a sight. She tightened her lacy shawl over her shoulders and shivered. 'Now, shall we read one more, something a bit happier, before I have to go?'

'You're going to a party?' Ruby asked.

'With Dr David?' Pearl added.

'We do like your gown an awful lot.' Ruby softly touched the pearl beads on Maddie's pale lilac silk and chiffon skirt, the long, fluttery sheer sleeves. 'It would be a beautiful wedding dress!'

'Silly. She would wear something grander to marry Dr David. Wouldn't you, Miss Maddie? Duchesse satin, and a ten-foot lace veil . . .' Pearl said.

Maddie laughed despite herself, despite her most secret dreams and deep doubts. 'I'd be a second-time bride, if I *did* marry. A nice suit and city hall, I should think.'

'Oh, no!' Pearl protested. 'Nothing like that for *you*. We're going to be bridesmaids, and we have plans, don't we, Ruby?' Ruby nodded emphatically. 'So does Father Malone, even though you're Epis . . . Epis . . .'

'Episcopalian,' Ruby supplied.

Maddie laughed even harder, her shoulders shaking, appalled and amused that her romantic life was the object of so many plans. 'Well, Dr David and I are both widowed, so a big to-do wouldn't look quite right, would it? And besides, my dears, he hasn't asked me and probably won't.' Did she *want* him to? She hadn't even decided yet.

'Oh, he will,' Ruby said confidently.

'You will both be the second to know, darlings.' She thought of Sofia and her royal court, all their velvet and antique lace and roses. Surely the girls imagined such a thing, too. But would Sofia have all that in her own wedding if she ran off now? And there was one thing very important to consider . . .

'Girls. What would you really think if Dr David came to live here?'

'We would love it!' Pearl said. 'There's too many women here with Eddie gone so much. It would be . . .'

'Lovely,' Ruby sighed. 'Like having a father again. A *proper* father this time.'

'Well, we should read one of your princess books before I go. You have certainly given me a great deal to think about.'

A few minutes later, she went across the garden from the Anayas' casita to the main house, leaving the girls tucked up and whispering under their quilts, the dogs sleeping on the rug beside their beds. Juanita was washing dishes at the sink, and quickly dried her hands to take the books and tuck them into the girls' school satchels.

'How was it, Señora Maddie?' she asked. 'I thought they would sleep through their naps into the night, but I forgot they never want to miss book time.'

'They think I don't realize they let Pansy and Buttercup up on to the beds as soon as I leave,' Maddie said. 'And I love book time, too.' She checked her reflection in the small mirror hanging by the back door. Her bobbed hair was smooth under a beaded bandeau, the short, fluttering chiffon sleeves of her gown perfectly straight for once. She reached for a tube of Cherries in the Snow lipstick. 'At least La Llorona seems to have put them off hanging about in the arroyos.'

Juanita nodded. 'That is very good. They have no business there, especially now that . . .' She blinked hard and turned away.

Maddie gently touched her arm, worried that maybe all of this was making Juanita remember her husband's end too much . . . Perhaps she shouldn't ask her to help with sleuthing anymore? But then Juanita would be hurt! 'I am sure no one would harm the girls. This was a very deliberate act toward one man.'

Juanita dashed her black sleeve quickly over her cheeks and turned back to the dishes. 'I know. But Pearl and Ruby – they are not really children any longer. They have to be careful. I worry so much . . .'

'So do I! But they have us, and Eddie, and the Sisters. And Gunther and David. And La Llorona. We won't let anything get past *us*.'

Juanita nodded, and yet Maddie saw clearly she was still worried. As Maddie was herself.

'You're going out, then, Señora Maddie?'

'Yes, to that new nightclub Gunther's been going on about. David sent a note saying he'd meet us there. Do I look like the bee's knees?' She gave a spin in her new gown, enjoying the way the beaded chiffon panels flared out. Maybe the twins were right, it would make a good wedding dress . . .

'You look beautiful. Dr David will be so proud.'

'The girls seem ready to break out their bridesmaids' frocks and march me down the cathedral aisle!'

Juanita tsked. 'Too many of those fashion magazines, those girls! I told them you have to be *very* sure before you marry again.'

'And what did they say?'

'They said, "How can Miss Maddie *not* be sure about Dr David? He's just like Henry Edwards in the movies."'

Maddie laughed. 'Well, he is that! Better, in fact. But I wouldn't be hiring the dressmakers and florists just yet.' A knock sounded at the door, and she kissed Juanita's cheek and tightened her fringed evening shawl. 'That will be Gunther. Don't wait up . . .'

Maddie and Gunther parked his Duesy near the museum, which was closed and quiet except for a few bright windows in the artists' studios, and turned toward the old building that semi-secretly housed the old Bennett speakeasy in its basement. Even though it was only a couple of blocks away from the Fiesta parties of the plaza, it felt very far indeed, the flashing lights and music just a muted echo.

Maddie held on to Gunther's arm as they made their way along the cracked walkway under the flickering glow of the few streetlights, the stars blinking in the clear sky. That end of Palace Street, past the cathedral park and the old Governor's Palace, beyond the store signs and the town's only Chinese restaurant, was a mix of business offices and rented flats, usually peaceful. Until the speakeasy first opened, under the management of the handsome, and ultimately very unreliable, Rob Bennett. For a brief while, it was the hottest ticket in town.

It'd been shut down for quite a while, the basement empty while the offices above were silent at night. Now Gunther said it was coming to life again, under the direction of Rob's sister, newly arrived from Denver.

Maddie could only hope she was very different from her siblings. A place to dress up and go dancing once in a while would be quite welcome.

They stopped at a two-story, nondescript building, with signs for a real-estate agent and a solicitor, and Gunther led her down a short flight of chipped stone steps to a peeling green-painted door. It all looked deserted, boarded-up. Yet when Gunther gave three short knocks, a tiny peephole slid open. Gunther waggled his fingers with a merry smile, and the door creaked away a mere crack and they were gestured inside.

It was like stepping into a different planet, one of warmth and soft light and laughter. Maddie gazed around in astonishment.

When Rob Bennett had the place, it was papered in dark

red to resemble an Old West saloon, with red leather banquettes at the little round tables grouped near the bar. Now the walls were painted a stylish eau de Nile, with gilt-framed mirrors hung along them to reflect the sparkling crowd, gold chairs upholstered in green and cream striped satin. Despite the basement room, the comparatively small space, it was light and airy and elegant, and Maddie's artistic senses applauded the effect.

There was still the polished, glasslike dance floor, crowded with couples draped in the height of fashion, sequins and fringe and lace, with a small stage at one end for the band, who played a lively rendition of 'I'll Build a Stairway to Heaven'. Along one wall stretched the bar, backed by shelves of bottles glowing like back-lit jewels, red, blue, green, gold. No Lightning there. White-jacketed waiters hurried past with trays of boeuf bourguignon, caviar on toast, and the scent of the rich food and the guests' French perfume, along with cigarette smoke, hung in the air.

'You're right, Gunther darling,' Maddie said. '*Très* swanky.'

A waitress in crisp black and white took their coats, and Maddie smoothed the skirt of her lavender-beaded gown before they made their way to the bar. Gunther pointed out a familiar figure across the room, Diego the Montoyas' major-domo, clad in an expensive evening suit and laughing with a fur-swathed matron. Gunther whispered he would just go have a little 'talky-to' with the man, and disappeared into the crowd.

Maddie recognized the bartender as a young man who sometimes worked with Eddie at La Fonda.

'Hello, Frankie!' she said. 'You do keep yourself busy.'

'Mrs Alwin!' he answered cheerfully, arranging a bouquet of bright cocktails on a silver tray. 'Sure I do. Gotta save up. What can I make for you?'

'That Gin Rickey looks yummy.' Maddie glanced across the room to see Gunther sitting at one of the tables with Diego, the two of them laughing. If anyone could get the man to confide in goings-on at the Montoya house, it was Gunther. 'That fella over there, in the nice suit, talking to Mr Ryder . . .'

Frankie nodded. 'Diego. Don't know his last name. He's been coming in here a fair bit since we opened. Big spender.'

'Is he now?' She wondered where he got all that 'big spending' money.

'Now, Frankie, do make this lady anything at all she wants, on the house,' a woman said as she slid in next to Maddie at the bar. She was petite, blonde, dressed in the height of fashion in pale blue tulle and silk, short and light as a cloud. 'If not for her, I might not even be running this swell business!' She held out a tiny diamond-bedecked hand. 'I'm Elspeth Bennett.'

Elspeth Bennett. She was clearly related to the Gruesome Siblings, with that golden hair, but her smile was open and kind.

'I'm Maddie Vaughn-Alwin.'

'I do owe you *masses* of apologies for what happened. Here, start with one of these Pink Ladies, our bartender's specialty, he really is a genius. I was lucky to find you, wasn't I, Frankie?' Elspeth said, with a giggle. 'I've been working in California and Denver, hadn't seen my awful brother in years. Then I found out he left this heavenly place empty, and I do hate to see good decor go to waste. Santa Fe seemed like a good fresh start. This town is really going places, isn't it?'

'It was a fresh start for me, too,' Maddie said.

'I did hate hearing about a murder here, though! Crime like that can be so bad for business, make people not want to go out and about.'

'Did you know Ricardo Montoya?'

Elspeth frowned. 'A little. When word slipped out I was opening up here, a few of your local businessmen came around wanting to invest. Mr Montoya was one of them.'

'Was he? I'm a bit surprised. He seemed to like doing the whole "upright pillar of the community" thing,' Maddie said, though she knew by then that Ricardo wasn't quite all he seemed.

Elspeth laughed. 'Don't they all? None of them want word to get out they're mixed up in stuff like booze, but they nearly all are. It's a nice little earner.' She waved her bejeweled hand at the sparkling crowd. 'I don't blame them. I'm a businesswoman myself. But I sure don't like people I work with to get hurt.'

'And did you? Work with Ricardo Montoya?'

She glanced away. 'In the end, no. He seemed like a nice enough fella, and of course everyone knows his family around here. But a little birdie whispered he wouldn't be good for the investment. Living beyond his means and all that.'

Maddie nodded, thinking of the disgruntled investors at the committee meeting. How angry *were* they all? 'You got out before he invested, then?'

'Sure. I'm no dummie. And I wanted to do this place up to suit myself.'

'You did a smashing job. The place is gorgeous, that's true.'

'I did a bit of a redecorate, you see. Some paint, some mirrors. Get rid of that bad – how would you say, bad energy? An exorcism? Someone said I should get someone out from the pueblo to burn some sage. Should I? Is that like an exorcism?'

Maddie laughed as she sipped at the admittedly excellent Pink Lady. 'I think you might be mixing two traditions there, but whatever you did so far it's working. You seem to be doing very well.'

'I like to make sure people have a good time,' Elspeth said, watching her crowd with narrowed eyes. 'But in a legit way! Drink and a dance, sure. I'd never dabble in drugs, like my brother, or ghosts, like my sister. I just want to make a decent living. Pretty ladies, handsome men, good music, some nice booze. Speaking of which . . .' She turned and called to her bartender. 'Are we out of the gin, sweetie?'

As Elspeth strode away to check on the gin situation, someone reached for Maddie's hand and kissed the back of her neck. She stiffened at first, ready to spin around and whack the Randy Andy, but then she realized – she knew that touch.

'So you made it at last,' she said, pretending indignation. 'Imagine, leaving a girl all alone in a place like this!'

David laughed, and kissed her again. He smelled delicious, of lemony soap and something like chocolate and his own warm David scent. 'I'd never do that to my best girl.'

'Only your second best, maybe?'

'How can I make it up to you?'

'A little dance?'

'You got it.' He took her hand and spun her onto the floor into a foxtrot.

David wasn't as smooth a dancer as Gunther, who was now twirling around the floor with the beautiful Laurencita Ellis, Diego nowhere to be seen. But Maddie did love being in his arms as they twirled and spun until the room was a diamond-blur around her. Waiters flowed in and out of the green baize door with their silver trays, their white jackets like a kaleido-scope. Murder and skullduggery did seem so far away.

'Swanky,' David said as he dipped her and made her giggle. 'A far cry from the hospital! And *you* look heavenly, like a luscious tea-cake, ready to eat up . . .'

'Yum!' She nibbled at his neck, making him laugh. What a glorious sound that laugh was, like the sunrise breaking through a dark night. 'I'm just happy we could lure you away for a few hours.'

'Well, I do have one teensy bit of hospital news you might be interested in . . .'

'Oh, do tell!'

'A new patient checked into Sunmount, an old business partner of Ricardo Montoya. Lots of hope for his health, but he does seem terribly worn down by his work.'

'Is his name George Marulis, by any chance?' Maddie asked.

'Yes, the same. How did you know?'

'Ricardo wanted his daughter to marry him, or used to. I heard a whisper they might have fallen out over something.'

'A marriage might have been meant to placate Mr Marulis about something. He does seem rather angry, it won't help his health.'

'Angry about what?' Maddie asked, deeply curious. Someone else with a secret grudge against Ricardo?

'Not sure, really. Psychiatry isn't my forte. He seemed very worked up about it when he first came, though, until the nurses hit him with morphine. A business deal, probably. And I think he would be strong enough still, if he caught someone by surprise.'

'Interesting. I always thought Ricardo Montoya was such

a respectable gentleman. Now it seems everyone was angry with him about something.' His family, business acquaintances. Who else?

David excused himself for a moment to say hello to another doctor he saw across the room, leaving Maddie alone to contemplate another Pink Lady. The door at the top of the stairs opened, letting in a blast of cool night air that cut through the cigarette smoke, a hint of guitar music from the plaza bandstand a few blocks away. Sofia Montoya stepped inside, dressed in the silver flapper frock she'd worn at El Delirio, Jake Silverstein holding her arm with one hand as he handed her a drink with the other. The two of them gave each other besotted little smiles as a raucous, laughing group piled in behind them, including the Fiesta Queen, Amalia Sanchez, her royal robes gone in favor of a pink satin gown beaded with pearls.

Sofia caught a glimpse of Maddie, and for an instant looked shocked, frightened, and very, very young. She whispered quickly to Jake, and threaded her way across the room to Maddie's side. Her perfume was Jicky, strong and expensive for a young lady.

'Mrs Alwin,' she said. 'I'm surprised to see you here.'

Maddie laughed. 'Surely not as surprised as I am to see *you*.'

Sofia's cheeks turned bright pink, and Maddie saw that under her daring gown, her rebellious romance, she was really still a sheltered young girl. She remembered too well her own turbulent emotions when she was Sofia's age, her wild desire to fly away from her parents' sheltered nest. What would Sofia do now that her wings were untethered?

'I know I should be with my mother while she's getting ready for the funeral, but she took a sleeping powder and went to bed early, and I so wanted to see Jake. You – you won't tell her, will you? I promise I'll go right home soon. Jake and I really aren't much for late nights. I can't wait until we can just sit in our own parlor and read together every night!'

'I'm not your nanny; I won't say a word. You want to go easy on those, though,' Maddie said, nodding at the royal-blue drink in Sofia's hand. 'So the engagement is on? Your mother doesn't object?'

Sofia smiled radiantly. 'Oh, no! Mama is an utter lamb. And she's so happy getting to see all her old friends again.'

Now that she was free? 'Friends like that sweet Señor Fernandez?'

'It was Papa who objected to Jake,' Sofia continued. 'He was so traditional. Didn't want to admit how the world is changing.' She took a long, defiant sip of her blue drink. 'If only he had realized that he might be happier making some changes, too.'

'What sort of changes? Did he maybe have a, well, a special friend of his own,' Maddie said carefully.

Sofia looked shocked. 'Papa? A mistress? No, I – I don't know, really, but I don't think so. No, not at all. He was so . . .'

'Traditional?'

'Yes! He seemed happiest at his business meetings, or at his *cofradia* at church. Not really with us.' She suddenly set her drink down with a clink and splash on the nearest table. 'Poor Papa. If only I could have helped him in some way.'

'Oh, Sofia, my dear. It was his job to help *you*. But do you mean you could have helped him on the night he died?'

'Yes, maybe. I don't know.' She frowned as she gazed across the room, as if lost in thought about that terrible night. 'That day, we'd had a quarrel, you see.'

'A quarrel? About your Jake?'

'Yes, of course. I told him if he separated me from my Jakie, I would take the veil!'

'Become a nun?' Maddie said, surprised. To go from nun to runaway bride seemed very dramatic.

'I had said I wanted to, before I met Jake, and maybe I would have done it then. But I sure wouldn't now. It was a dumb thing to say. Papa would have much rather I became a nun than married Jake.'

Yet being a nun wouldn't have brought Ricardo the business help it seemed he needed. Not like a match with Mr Marulis might have. 'That was the last time you saw your father?'

Tears shimmered in Sofia's eyes. 'Yes. We said such hurtful things to each other! If I had just known . . .'

Maddie found a handkerchief in her beaded evening bag

and handed it to Sofia, who loudly blew her nose. 'Did you stay home with your mother that night?'

Sofia dabbed at her eyes, and shook her head. 'I'm ashamed to say I snuck out with Jake, went to the Fiesta dance and then drove up in the foothills. I didn't get home until very late, climbed in a window by the pool.'

So Sofia wouldn't know where her mother and brother were that night, either. 'Did you see anyone else around your house?'

Sofia's brow wrinkled in thought. 'No. I assumed Mama was asleep, her door was closed. And so was Papa's.' That confirmed they didn't sleep together, even if Ricardo didn't have a mistress on the side. 'I knocked on Juan-Antonio's door, but he didn't answer. Maybe he was out, too? He used to tell me everything, but now he's so secretive.'

Maddie thought of her own brother in New York, how he would never, ever have confided in his sister about his 'lads' nights out'. 'You and Juan-Antonio are close?'

'Oh, yes! I can tell him anything, he understands. We both want to – wanted to escape so much. Be ourselves, you know? Live our lives the way we want!' She seemed to realize she'd said too much, and bit her lip. 'He's a good friend.'

'And what does Juan-Antonio want to do? Not go to college and join your father's business? I can understand that.'

'He just likes to paint,' Sofia said quietly.

'I do know that feeling! My parents didn't approve of my dream to be an artist, either.'

'He says when that need to create is inside of you, it won't be cut out again.' Sofia's eyes suddenly widened. 'Oh! Yes. I thought I *did* see someone that night.'

'Who was it?'

'Diego. My father's manservant. I glimpsed him at one of the casitas just beyond the pool, but he was in an evening suit and a cloak thing, so I thought I was imagining things, that it must be Juan-Antonio. They're a similar height. But his hair is lighter than my brother's.'

Maddie glanced around the club, but didn't see Diego anywhere now. He did seem to pop up everywhere. Could he have been following Ricardo, or even been mistaken for

Juan-Antonio by someone else? 'What do you think he was doing?'

Sofia sniffed. 'Snooping, probably. I've caught him doing that before. I don't know why my father kept him on.' She waved at Jake, smiling again. 'I have to go, Mrs Alwin! You really won't tell my mother, about seeing me here? I promise it's not my usual sort of spot at all. Jake and I were just curious about it all.'

Maddie nodded, and watched Sofia hurry off to her fiancé. He kissed her cheek, and they beamed at each other. Everyone did seem better off in some way now that Ricardo was gone. But what was Diego about? She hoped Gunther had found out something.

She finished her drink and went in search of David.

'Ready to go?' he asked.

'Oh, yes. I need a little fresh air.' All the gin and cigarette smoke were making things so much more confusing than they already were! David fetched their coats, and took her arm as they strolled out into the night, whispering together. The night was chilly but beautiful, and being with David made her feel steadier. They kissed next to the gate to her house, and he promised to come around the next day as soon as his visits were done at the hospital. He walked away whistling, the music fading behind him and making her smile.

She didn't want to go inside yet, not with everything she'd heard at the speakeasy still whirling around in her head. She saw a tiny red glow on Gunther's portal, the end of his cigarette, and went through the connecting gate of their gardens to see what he'd learned from the beauteous Diego.

'Elspeth certainly has made an elegant spot,' she said, sitting down in one of the wicker chairs and kicking her court-heeled shoes off her aching feet. Gunther handed her a glass of something pink and unidentifiable, but yummy.

'Well, I wouldn't be at all surprised if he was in on a spot of blackmail of his employer,' Gunther said. 'Though I can't say what it was about yet. He certainly had the cash to splash around, more than any major-domo I can imagine! He said Ricardo was generous, and he certainly will miss him. I can't imagine he would kill the golden goose in that instance. And he said he was at a party that night, lots of people to see him.' He lit another cigarette, and laughed. 'He even asked me if I was hiring! As if I could afford to keep anyone but me in pearl shirt studs and gold cufflinks.'

'Not to mention your cravats.' They sat together quietly, companionably, for a long moment, listening to the night-bird calls around them. 'Oh, Gunther. You really are just like the brother I always wanted. Someone to get into mischief with me.'

He laughed again, sounding surprised and pleased. 'Am I, Madcatkins? I thought you already had a brother.'

'Oh, yes. Henry. Someone mentioned him lately; maybe that's why I thought of it. But we're so different we might as well be from two planets. I'm not sure how we have the same parents.' She thought of her brother, his brilliantined mustache and starched shirts, his way of talking and pontificating for hours and not saying anything at all. 'But you and me . . .'

Gunther nodded, and stubbed out the cigarette in a cut-glass ashtray. 'We *are* sympatico, aren't we, darling? I've always been so happy you moved in next door.'

'Me, too.' She tucked her feet beneath her, and thought about how this whole thing around Ricardo Montoya seemed to come down to belonging, to finding one's true place, true happiness. Fitting in, and not fitting in. Love, maybe, but not the kind that was good for you. 'Have you ever *really* been in love? Mad love?'

Gunther frowned, and reached for his Cartier cigarette case. He studied the inscription inside the lid for a long moment. Maddie wondered if the case was from a lost love, and glanced away. 'I'm sorry, Gunther dearest. I shouldn't pry.'

'Of course you should. Who else can you talk to but your Uncle Gunther? Is something amiss with the dishy doctor, then?'

'Not at all. And it isn't *mad* love, either. It's – well, it's nice. Very, very nice.' She smiled a secret little smile to remember his good-night kiss. The strong, steady feeling of his arm under her hand.

'It sounds perfect, darling.'

'It feels perfect. Maybe that's why I worry.'

'Ah, I see. Don't want to jinx it all.'

'Something like that, I suppose. It hurt so very much when Pete died, and I – I don't want to do that again,' she whispered. She hadn't quite realized that fear until just that moment.

'Oh, Maddie my darling.' Gunther reached out to take her hand. 'Has your Dr David given some indication he wants to leave you?'

'No, not at all. It's just . . .'

'His work? He is quite the busy hero with all his patients. They do adore him and need him.'

'Oh, it's just me being a silly-billy.'

'You? A silly? Never! But it is quite understandable. When we have a loss, or a few, and we manage to pick ourselves up – well, resilience does get exhausting.'

Maddie thought of Catalina and Ricardo, and wondered how much resilience had been called upon in their life together. Had it all just snapped, like a cord tweaked once too often? She sighed, and leaned against Gunther's shoulder. 'But what choice do we have but to pick ourselves up?'

'None at all, darling. Not if we want to truly create, truly love.' He kissed her forehead, and they looked out into the dark garden together. 'I think I *did* love once. Maybe twice. But they didn't last.'

'Oh, Gunther,' Maddie whispered, and tightened her hand on his.

'Not to worry! You found your Dr David, and you had better be brave and hold on to him. I shall do the same one day, I'm sure. And you and I will always have each other.'

'Yes. Each other.' Holding on to the people she loved – that was all that was important now.

NINE

The sounds of a parade nearly overwhelmed the tolling cathedral bells the next morning when Maddie walked with the twins to school. Much as Juanita predicted, they had no desire to venture near *any* arroyos after reading about La Llorona, which meant taking the longer walk. Not that Maddie minded that. Even though her head was still a bit muzzy from the late night, she had errands of her own waiting for the day, and the clear, golden sunlight and the piñon-scented breeze cleared her thoughts wonderfully.

In her handbag was a note from Catalina, asking if she could come to the Montoya house that afternoon to do a few sketches to help with the portrait until Catalina could come to the studio again. Maddie was glad of the chance to see her again – and maybe have a good snoop around the house, if the opportunity presented itself. She thought of Sofia at the nightclub, dancing so happily with her young man, of George Marulis at Sunmount, of what Gunther said about Diego and his oodles of money. The Montoya family weren't quite what they showed the outside world, that was for sure.

But then again, she thought, whose family really were? The Vaughns certainly weren't.

Ruby excitedly caught her hand to show her a hat in a window, making hints about wedding garb again, and Maddie laughed. Her real family were right here, the family she'd made herself from her own choices. Her parents were like Ricardo Montoya, doing what was expected, what everyone else said they should. Maybe Sofia and Juan-Antonio, and Catalina, too, just didn't want to do that anymore. How far would they go to escape?

'Can we go to the plaza after school, Miss Maddie?' Pearl asked. The sounds of the parade, drums and horns and laughter, still sounded in the crisp morning air, bringing a life and gaiety to the sleepy town. 'They say people will be dancing on the plaza! And there will be booths selling popcorn and candy apples, and tamales.'

'If your mother says it's OK,' Maddie said. Juanita was strict about healthy meals and bedtimes and homework, but she never begrudged her children treats, either. And Maddie wouldn't mind a bit of popcorn herself.

'Hooray!' the twins cried, and skipped toward the school. It seemed the frights of La Llorona were forgotten.

Sister Mary Cecilia stood on the steps, ushering the last of the girls inside. Pearl and Ruby were nearly late, which Juanita would *not* like, and Maddie urged them ahead as she stopped to chat with Sister Mary Cecilia. She remembered the sister had once taught Sofia.

'How are they doing in their classes, Sister Mary Cecilia?' she asked. 'When I'm not slowing them down terribly!'

'They've been doing quite well!' Sister Mary Cecilia said cheerfully. 'Pearl is especially adept in her science classes . . .'

'You've been at Loretto several years, haven't you, Sister?' Maddie asked, after they chatted about the twins for a while.

Sister Mary Cecilia pulled a face and laughed. 'More than I care to remember! When I arrived, Santa Fe was just a couple of dirt roads.'

'You've taught so many girls, then.'

'Oh, yes. The Luhans, and the Oteros . . .'

'And Sofia Montoya, I think?'

Sister Mary Cecilia nodded sadly, the white edges of her wimple rippling. 'Yes, that poor girl. To lose her father like that! Señor Montoya was more involved with his daughter's education than most fathers are. Always coming to Mother Superior's office to ask about her studies and behavior.'

'Was she a good pupil, then?'

'Wonderful. Smart, quiet, devout. I think she's the only pupil I've ever had who never required a moment's punishment! No standing in corners for her. She always won the good manners medal at the end of the year. I did worry sometimes that maybe she was a bit *too* quiet.'

There was a burst of chatter and loud laughter beyond the

open doors of the school, making Maddie and Sister Mary Cecilia smile. 'I would think the quiet ones would be a relief!'

'Of course we emphasize manners and proper behavior for our girls. Such important qualities to help them in life! And Sofia never gave us a complaint. Her parents would not have liked that, and they were – still are – important benefactors to the school.'

'Sofia does seem like a nice young lady,' Maddie said, and thought of how she danced at the nightclub, lighter, more full of laughter than she had been before. 'I suppose she might get married soon. I thought I heard a rumor of the sort.'

'Girls from families like the Montoyas do tend to marry rather young. I'm sure she had suitors, though I've heard nothing for certain. Our old students often come back to talk to Mother Superior when they get engaged. Give us news, ask for advice. It's very sweet! We do love hearing about their lives.' She frowned in thought. 'It's funny – I didn't remember until just now. Sofia used to say she'd like to be a nun! We didn't sense she had a true vocation, but perhaps she saw it as a . . .' Her words trailed away.

'As a what, Sister?'

'I don't know. As an escape of some sort. Some girls do see taking vows as something of the kind. They don't realize that being a nun just brings *more* of the world's troubles to your door! Sofia, as sweet as she was – I'm not sure she would have been strong enough.'

Maddie remembered the club again, Sofia dancing and laughing, and wondered if Sister Mary Cecilia didn't under-estimate her. Or maybe Sofia had just shed a mask at last. 'Would her parents have allowed her to be a nun, if she truly had a calling?'

'Her mother, certainly. Catalina Montoya is a pious woman. Her father, hmm, probably, if word got around that Sofia wished it. Santa Fe, the Montoyas' Santa Fe, is not a place where a person could ignore the Church. Now that I think about it, maybe dear Sofia was craftier than I thought! She must have known they would feel that, too.'

And it was one way Sofia could have gotten her own wishes

– for a while, anyway. Now she was free of the need for that.
'And her brother? Did he go to school at St Michael's?'

'Of course. He was a good student, as well. Not as steady
as his sister. Mathematics in particular was difficult for him,
and I'm sure his parents worried about that. Señor Montoya
was always so insistent to Brother Botolph that Juan-Antonio
must go to university in the East before he took over the family
business! I believe he *has* been admitted somewhere – Yale?
– but it took rather a lot of extra tutoring.'

'Juan-Antonio didn't like that? Going off to university?'

'Brother Botolph was sure he preferred art and music. Juan-
Antonio was good at both. Sofia envied that; her sketching
was proficient at best. But Juan-Antonio was talented. He gave
us a lovely painting he'd created of the cathedral at sunset
against a cloudy sky, and it still hangs in the foyer of the
Brothers' refectory.'

'I should like to see it,' Maddie said. It seemed both the
Montoya siblings were free now. Free to follow their own
dreams.

The final bell rang, and Sister Mary Cecilia excused herself
to go inside and shut the doors. Maddie decided to walk to
the Montoya house, even though it was a bit far. It was a
beautiful autumn day, warm and golden, and she got a bag of
popcorn from one of the booths on the plaza. As she happily
munched and walked, waving to people she knew, she thought
of what Sister Mary Cecilia said about the Montoya siblings
and their dreams.

It was nothing she hadn't seen from the Montoyas before,
that Sofia and Juan-Antonio weren't happy with their father's
expectations, but it was interesting that Sofia was willing to
go so far as to become a nun to get away from them. But
would she really have been able to chop a full-grown dead
body up and carry it to the arroyo? She was a petite girl. Her
Jake was not.

The gates were open to the estate, so Maddie strolled right
in. The gardens were quiet, seemingly empty. Diego wasn't
there, but Mrs Hurst opened the door again, a strangely cheerful
smile greeting her.

'Mrs Alwin, isn't it? It's good to see you again,' she said, ushering Maddie into the foyer. 'Mrs Montoya was ever so much steadier after your last visit.'

'Was she really? I'm glad I could help.'

'Oh, yes! She's been coming downstairs for her meals, listening to the gramophone, sending out for lending library books. I do worry about her sometimes, she doesn't really seem to have any friends, which is very sad for a lady in her position.'

'But she and Señor Montoya always seemed to be attending events! Dinners, committee meetings, Church things . . .'

'Oh, yes, indeed,' Mrs Hurst said, her lips pursing. 'He did like to show his face around town, didn't he? Someone of importance and all that. But I will tell you this, in confidence – everyone they socialized with were *his* friends. People who could help him, you know? In fact . . .' She leaned closer and said in a near-whisper, 'In fact, Mrs Alwin, I did hear the two of them arguing last week. Not that I tried, mind you; I haven't kept my job here so long by being a listening Lorna. But them raising their voice was a strange thing. Usually anything important here is very hush-hush.'

Fascinating. 'What did they argue about?' Maddie whispered.

'Well, it was just that, wasn't it? Friends. Mrs Montoya said *he* was always off with his friends, doing whatever he liked, while she saw no one at all. She wasn't allowed to so much as have tea with someone he didn't approve of, someone who couldn't be of use to him. She said she didn't fancy living like that now, and she would tell everyone that . . .' Mrs Hurst stopped abruptly, pursing her lips even tighter as if to keep the words from flying out.

'Tell everyone – what?' Maddie asked, on tenterhooks. Who could imagine the elegant, contained Catalina *arguing*?

'I don't really know, Mrs Alwin. There was a terrible cracking sound, almost as if he might have hit her, and she cried out. Now that *was* strange, he was a stern man but not one to behave like that.'

'That brute,' Maddie gasped. She certainly hadn't especially liked Ricardo, he was too old-fashioned and such, but Mrs Hurst was right. He hadn't seemed the sort to hit his wife.

Then again, one never really knew. And what *friends* could they have been so upset about? Did he perhaps treat his children the same way, bullying them physically? Who else had he bullied, possibly beyond bearing?

'It would be nice if your sweet Mrs Anaya could come back sometime, Priscilla was ever so much better after she left,' Mrs Hurst said. 'No more sniffling into her apron. You and your friends seem to do us a world of good!'

A burst of laughter, sparkling and merry, flowed through the half-open sitting room door, warm and easy as two people who had known each other a long time could be. It looked like the days of acrimonious quarrels and sad silences in that house were at an end. Mrs Hurst led her through the foyer into the sitting room, where some of the heavy, dark furniture had been moved out and new, lighter, cream-upholstered chairs moved in, along with untidy stacks of magazines, and a phonograph and stacks of records. Maddie saw that Catalina was with Señor Fernandez, her childhood suitor.

It did look like Catalina still had one real friend of her own. The two of them were laughing, their heads bent close together as they looked at a magazine. Catalina still wore black, of course, the rich sheen of satin that fell to her knees and draped elegantly over the shoulders. Instead of pearls, she wore a strand of turquoise and coral beads, a spot of bright color, and her usually tightly pinned hair flowed into a soft knot at the base of her neck, held with a carved ivory comb.

She leaned closer to Señor Fernandez, laughing, a silvery, musical sound that was true mirth.

'Mrs Alwin to see you, madame,' Mrs Hurst announced, and Catalina sat back on the sofa, seemingly unfazed to be found having some fun. She didn't move too far from Señor Fernandez.

'Oh, Maddie, thank you so much for coming,' Catalina said. 'It's been much too quiet here. You have met my friend Señor Fernandez, of course. He said you're on the masked ball committee together! We have been friends for simply ages. He brought some new records to cheer me up. Have you heard of someone called – Jelly Roll? His songs are quite delightful.'

'Of course I know Señor Fernandez. How nice to see you again! And you look so much better today, Catalina, I'm so glad to see.' Maddie took off her hat and gloves, and started to unpack her sketchbooks and pencils from her handbag. It would really be good to capture a bit of Catalina for the painting; she looked lighter now, younger by years.

She looked like she was happy.

As Maddie set up her art supplies on a low table, she surreptitiously watched the two of them chatting on the sofa. She remembered hearing that they had once been childhood sweethearts, and it looked like that time was coming back as they leaned closer to each other, so comfortable together.

'But we must let Maddie get on with her work!' Catalina said with a laugh. 'How shall I sit? Like so?'

'Yes, Catalina, just sit like that, hands in your lap, chin up and to the left just a smidge, a hint of a smile. As if you see something absolutely fascinating in the distance!' Maddie instructed as she got her charcoal pencil ready.

'Shall I go so you can get some work done?' Señor Fernandez asked.

'Oh, no, André, we have so much to talk about after all this time! He shall sit very quietly there in the corner, like a wee tiny mouse,' Catalina said, teasingly shooing Señor Fernandez off his chair.

He laughed as he retreated to a seat near the window. 'I admit I am very curious about the art process.'

'Of course you must stay! The more the merrier,' Maddie said, taking one long sweep of her pencil down the paper. 'I'm sure you can give me some details to add a bit of depth to the portrait, since you've known each other so long. To show the real *you*, Catalina!'

'The real me is dull indeed, Maddie! Paint me as glamorous and mysterious.'

'I think it will be more – elegant, as you are,' Maddie said.

'Elegant is not so bad, Catalina,' André said. 'And you truly are. Our own Lillian Gish in Santa Fe!'

'Oof, after that mischief we all saw on the film set, poor Mr Luther being killed and all, I dare not even try to be actressy,' Catalina giggled. *Giggled!* 'Though I wouldn't mind actually going to the theater to see a movie or two. I've never done that, it sounds fascinating.'

'What, never?' Maddie said, adding a bit of shade to the drape of Catalina's sketched skirt. 'Don't your children see them? Sofia is so pretty, maybe she'd like to be in the flicks!'

Catalina laughed. 'No, no. They do enjoy movies, but they have their own ideas. Ideas were always something Ricardo was against as much as films.'

'Oh? I think my parents would have agreed, sadly,' Maddie said.

'Sofia told me this morning she *will* marry the Silverstein boy, and if she can't she will take the veil. Though I never could imagine her as a nun. And Juan-Antonio wants to go to some art school, not Harvard at all. *Dios mío.*'

'Will they really do those things now?'

Catalina shook her head, her gaze suddenly very far away, as if she tried to picture the new future. 'I don't really know. I have no objection to Sofia's marriage. They say Mr Silverstein is a good man, a hard worker, ambitious, and I am sure he'll find his way with Sofia's help. My girl was always stronger than she looked.'

'Even though he is not of your faith?' Maddie asked carefully.

Catalina glanced at Señor Fernandez. 'There are so many fine Jewish families here in Santa Fe, and there have been for many years. Successful, respectable families. The Staabs and Seligmans. She could do much worse, and if his family is prepared to accept her, I shall do the same.'

'And our friends wouldn't dare snub them once they are married,' André said, stretching out his long legs as if he was perfectly comfortable in that sitting room. 'With the Montoyas, the Fernandezes, the Gomezes behind them, they will do very well.'

'My aunt married an Anglo man when I was a girl,' Catalina said. 'She only lived down the street, but we weren't allowed to talk to her for years. How I hated that. But that was long ago! It's all different now. I shall not stand in the way of her happiness. I am the parent now, what I say is what goes.' And she did sound very different than she had just a week before. Determined and decisive.

'And what of Juan-Antonio's ideas, *querida*?' André asked.

Catalina sighed, and smoothed her skirt. 'How can he really want to give up Harvard? He worked so hard for it all, all those mathematics tutors. Ricardo was so adamant that our son take over the business, and for that he needed a solid education, contacts everywhere. Art was a mere hobby, good enough in its place, to show everyone how *cultured* we are. Have you seen his work, Maddie? You would be able to tell me if it is good.'

'I haven't. I heard he has a painting hanging at the refectory, and Sister Mary Cecilia said everyone admires it. I can ask around at the Art Museum, maybe look at his portfolio, if he'd let me.'

'Oh, yes, do. Then I can decide if he is talented enough to leave Harvard and go to this art school. If he is *not* truly talented, then it must remain a hobby, I think. I can't have him *dabbling*. If he has real potential, then so be it.'

'I can't say you're wrong,' Maddie answered. 'Art is no easy profession at all, but if he must do it, if it's his soul, then he won't be turned away.'

'May I see what you've done so far, Mrs Alwin?' André asked.

'Certainly.' Maddie showed them her sketchbooks, the studies she'd been doing to finish Catalina's portrait as well as some mountainscapes she'd been trying.

Maddie excused herself to 'visit the ladies' necessary', and left Catalina and Señor Fernandez chatting happily over the tea.

The upstairs corridors were quiet, and as she peeked around she realized she could have a wee little glance before she was missed in the sitting room. Just see what those letters on Ricardo's desk, which she had glimpsed on her last visit, had to say.

The study was quite tidy, and she remembered no one was allowed to clean in there, so surely there were a few things of Ricardo's no one had seen before. She carefully slid open the top drawer of the desk, and found business letters there, a few getting increasingly irate about monies owed, which confirmed what she'd heard at the committee meeting. Tucked underneath was a yellowing envelope, and inside were a few photographs.

They, too, were fading, not images of his family but of Ricardo as a young man, with thick, dark hair and old-fashioned round spectacles. They seemed to all be of his college days, grinning with other fellas beside a rowing boat, in crisp blazers, holding pints in a bar. How different he looked then, so happy!

In one, a figure stood just behind Ricardo, a bit blurry as if he'd moved just as the photographer snapped, but there was something familiar about the tall man, the brush of hair . . .

'Maddie! Are you there!' Catalina called from downstairs, and Maddie quickly shoved the photos in the desk. She'd have to sketch out what she remembered later.

Catalina was alone in the sitting room when Maddie returned, studying the garden through the open glass door and humming a soft tune. 'Jelly Roll's Blues', Maddie thought, the record Señor Fernandez brought her.

'Your house is lovely, Catalina,' Maddie said. 'The painted tiles in the hallway are especially lovely, and what you did with the colors . . .'

'Thank you, dear Maddie! I do appreciate your artistic eye.' Catalina returned to the sofa and poured out more tea. 'But I'm thinking of making a few changes. Giving it all a more – modern look, maybe. Yes. I've never been *modern*, it might be fun. Perhaps I should get one of those little Pekinese dogs that are so stylish now?'

Maddie laughed, and then remembered the little hairs stuck to Ricardo's sleeve. 'You don't have a pet now?'

'No. Ricardo never liked them, you see, they shed on the furniture . . .'

As Maddie approached the turn of the street to her own house, thoughts of Catalina and Señor Fernandez and the past and secrets swirling in her mind, she caught a glimpse of a familiar figure in the distance and her heart did a little dance.

'David! Darling, are you here to see me? What a lovely

surprise,' she called, hurrying to catch up with him. She went up on tiptoe to kiss him, wrapping her arms around him and squeezing until he laughed.

'Juanita promised to feed me if I came by today,' he said. They linked arms and strolled slowly toward the house.

'Oh, I see, you have to be bribed by Juanita's cooking,' she teased. 'Well, I'll take what I can get to see you.'

'Where were you off to?'

'To see Catalina Montoya.'

'How was she?'

'Better than you might expect. She's doing her hair in a new style, and talking about getting a Pekinese! Her friend Señor Fernandez was there.'

'A Pekinese, eh? Sounds ominous. Find anything else interesting?'

'What makes you think I was a snoop, David Cole?' she said, pretending to be indignant.

He laughed. 'Because I know you by now.'

'So you do. Too well, I'd say!'

'Why don't you come out to Sunmount tomorrow, chat with George Marulis?'

'The man you said had business dealings go sour with Ricardo Montoya? Who might have married Sofia? Is he terribly ill? I would like to hear his story, but I don't want to be a nuisance. Not *too* big a nuisance, anyway.'

'It's early days yet. With some rest and care, he'll be right as rain. He'd probably like to talk about it a bit, it all seems to prey on his mind rather.'

'But when did he arrive there? Before or after the murder?'

David thoughtfully rubbed at his bearded chin. 'The day after, I think.'

'So he might have had time to do it.' Maddie thought it over, and nodded. 'I will come, then. Maybe I can persuade Gunther to loan me his Duesy again . . .'

But when she got home, she found a note from Gunther asking her for another adventure first. *Want to see if we can find the beauteous Diego the major-domo at the GR tonight, darling? Could be fun!*

TEN

Maddie had always rather secretly yearned to glimpse inside the Golden Rooster Club, it looked so bland and windowless and paint-peeling from the outside and yet was whispered about as something in a film, mysterious and smoky-glamorous, with the best booze. So when Gunther suggested they track down Diego there, maybe find out what really went on in the Montoya house, she jumped at the chance.

Now – well, it was all a tad bit disappointing, if she was honest. She'd expected something like the fancy Bennett speakeasy, spangled and sparkly. Yet, even though it was very large, an old warehouse that once housed grain moving through the state, it was so dimly lit she could barely see more than two feet in front of her. She'd taken care to dress properly, in a pants suit borrowed from Gunther and tilted black hat, but surely it wouldn't have mattered what she wore, no one could see her anyway.

It was pleasant, though, and she could definitely see why Gunther enjoyed it. Quiet music from a trio at the end of the room, a dance floor, modern, interesting art on the walls.

And the couples who shared drinks at the small round tables, who circled the little dance floor, whispered and laughed, were almost all men. Men who in the daylight might pretend not to even know each other, but there they could just be themselves. No one stared, or gave any indication at all that they knew anyone who slipped in the door. As soon as they slipped out again, the amnesia would set in.

Maddie squeezed Gunther's hand, and thought of how he'd spent his life taking refuge in places like this, yearning to be himself just as she did. She knew he wanted real love now, wanted to settle down. Would he find someone like that here?

He smiled down at her, and squeezed her fingers back. They

always seemed to know what the other was thinking, what the silent sympathy meant. 'Come on, Mads darling, let me buy you the best gin and tonic in town,' he said.

'I will definitely take you up on that.' They made their way to the small curved bar tucked in a corner of the vast room. It wasn't flashy like at Bennett's, no sparkling mirrors, but the bottles lined up on the rough pine shelves were very top-drawer indeed.

The bartender, a tall, stocky figure in shirtsleeves and a red velvet waistcoat, turned to them, and Maddie saw to her surprise that it was a woman. Her dark hair was chopped into a sleek Eton crop; spectacles perched on her nose and a cigar-ette dangled from her red-lipsticked mouth.

'Haven't seen you here in an age, sweetie,' she said around her cigarette, reaching out to enthusiastically pump Gunther's hand. 'Thought you'd given up on us!'

'Never! Your cognac is always too good to refuse, Eva,' Gunther said, helping Maddie up on to one of the high stools. 'And I heard you got in a fantastic gin shipment.'

'All the way from Canada! Two coming right up, then.' Eva poured and stirred two icy G&Ts, quick and efficient and sleek.

Maddie took a sip, and sighed. 'Superlative,' she sighed, and it was. Icy and crisp and green-herbal flavored.

Gunther slipped a shockingly large wad of cash across the scarred bartop. 'I'm looking for someone, name of Diego. Very handsome, tall, with yummy brown eyes. And snake-y hips.'

Eva laughed, and lit a new cigarette off the end of the old one. 'Aren't we all looking for that, sweetie?'

'Indeed. But I have no amorous or nefarious intentions tonight. Just a few questions for the gentleman.'

Eva frowned suspiciously. 'Who is it you're after, then?'

'A fellow named Diego. Worked for the Montoyas before the shocking events this week. I know I've seen him here a time or two.'

Eva pocketed the cash. 'Sure, I know him. Everyone does. A real looker. Big spender, too, especially lately.' She glanced around, eyes narrowed. 'Haven't seen him here tonight, but he'll be around later, I'm sure. Why don't you and your friend grab a table, have a bottle of this cognac, and you can wait. On the house.' Her hard expression softened as she gently touched Gunther's sleeve. 'Don't be a stranger here so long, sweetie. We miss you.'

'Ah, and I miss you, too, Eva,' Gunther said with a laugh. 'I miss your cognac the *mostest*.'

Gunther turned to chat with someone to his other side as Eva fetched the bottle from under the bar, and Maddie studied a blank stretch of whitewashed wall above the shelves. 'A mural would really brighten things up there, you know, Miss Eva. Maybe a classical scene, a Dionysian dance or Zeus's feast.'

Eva squinted up at the wall doubtfully. 'You really think so?'

'Maddie is one of the finest artists in Santa Fe,' Gunther said. He glanced at someone out of the corner of his eye, a little, secret smile fluttering across his face. 'You'd be lucky to get her to take a commission, Eva! She's doing a portrait of Catalina Montoya right now.'

'Hmm. So that's why you're asking about someone from the Montoyas' place?'

'Something like that,' Maddie said. 'You do know what happened to Ricardo Montoya?'

Eva snorted, and reached for the bottle of gin. 'Everyone does. Not many things like that go on in Santa Fe, not so you see anyway.' She tapped at her nose. 'Working here, you gotta keep a lot under your hat, you know? Forget lots of stuff.'

'I would imagine so,' Maddie murmured. She longed to ask Eva more, but the woman turned away to serve more customers and Gunther led Maddie to a table tucked beside the dance floor. He soon drifted away into a foxtrot himself, so Maddie was alone, sipping her cognac, when she saw Diego come into the room. Oh, yes, he was a 'looker', better than any movie star with his patent-polished dark hair and sharp-cut gray suit. Maddie tossed back the last of her cognac and strolled up to tap him on the shoulder.

'Dance with me,' she said.

He did not look terribly surprised when he glanced down at her, which disappointed her a bit. She always longed to be the mysterious femme fatale of a film, yet she was too much *Maddie* to be so mysterious.

'Sure,' he said, and took her hand to spin her on to the floor. He was a very good dancer, of course, smooth and lithe. 'You're that artist lady at Señora Montoya's. Never would have thought I'd see *you* here.'

'I came with a friend.'

'You aren't really the sort, are you?'

'The sort?'

He glanced her over quite thoroughly, until Maddie was afraid she was blushing like a schoolgirl. 'You don't have enough of – something. And too much of other things.'

She laughed. 'And here I thought my trousers were such a disguise!'

He twirled her around until she was dizzy. 'It does look snazzy, no mistake.'

'And so do you. Look snazzy. I love your suit. Brooks Brothers, isn't it?'

'Good eye.'

'It must pay well, being a – what was it? Major-domo?' Maddie remembered what Juanita found out from her cousin at the Montoyas', about the suspected thefts.

He frowned. 'Not bad, no.'

'Will you be looking for new employment now?'

He spun them to one of the small tables in a dark corner, and twirled her into the chair. He sat down across from her and took a pack of expensive cigarettes from inside his jacket pocket. 'Who are you, really, señorita? You seem pretty snoopy for a painter.'

'But that's just what I am. A painter. And a friend of Catalina. I feel a bit sorry for her.'

'Don't we all? But I wouldn't feel *too* bad for her, she's better off now. So, you are – what? Looking into this murder for her?'

'Something like that. I'm a big fan of Christie, you see, and Chesterton stories.'

'Fascinating.' He lit the cigarette with a silver lighter, and exhaled a plume of smoke. He really did look like a film star. He was wasted in Santa Fe. 'I rather enjoy a good detective story myself. I will tell you something, then, because for some reason I like you. You are quite – unusual. I don't see that very often.'

'I'll take that as a compliment.'

'You should.'

'And I would say you're pretty unusual yourself.'

'So I am. And I can easily find employment when I want it. Things were not so nice at the Montoyas' house anymore, anyway. You see everyone here tonight? That state senator over there? The silver-mine owner back here? I could get a job with any of them. I do a bit of this, a bit of that, make myself useful.'

'Anywhere, huh?' Maddie could see that. Diego was assuredly one of life's survivors.

'Well, not just with *anyone* in town, of course. There are those who fear scandal too much. Just like people everywhere.'

'Oh, yes. I'm from New York. I know all about secrets and silences.'

Diego leaned closer and whispered, 'Do you know a man named Mateo Otero?'

Maddie thought of the man at the committee meeting, the one so quickly angered by mention of Ricardo. 'I met him once at a Fiesta ball committee.'

'What did you think of him?' Diego stared down at the ashtray in front of him.

Maddie shrugged. 'Not much, I guess. He seemed like a lot of other business-type men from old families around here. A bit set in his ways. He didn't seem to like Ricardo. Something about business deals.'

He laughed. 'Business, huh? He was afraid his son, Mateo junior, was in some trouble with Juan-Antonio Montoya. Tsk tsk.'

'Juan-Antonio?' Maddie whispered. If Señor Otero wanted to protect his son, and he thought Ricardo was somehow in his way . . .

'I know. Silly. Juan-Antonio doesn't think about anything but art, really. Some people do not see so deeply, look behind things, as you and I do.'

Maddie studied him carefully. 'And did you and Juan-Antonio happen to – appreciate art together?' If that was the cause of Diego's sudden wealth, some sort of blackmail over the Montoya heir?

Diego laughed even harder, his whole glorious Renaissance-god face lit up. 'Me and Juan-Antonio? I posed for him once or twice, that is all. He seems to have talent, though I'm not educated enough to say for sure. People like me, we just have to make a living where we can. Boys like Juan-Antonio, with their silly young heads in the clouds, are no use.'

'But you know lots of things about the Montoya house, I think.'

He shrugged. 'I have to know things about all sorts of people. Keep my eyes and ears open. Then I store it all here.' He tapped at his forehead. 'That's the only way it's of use to me. And now that Ricardo is dead . . .'

'Now what?'

His expression shifted, becoming something sincere, intense. Oh, yes, Maddie thought. He was wasted off a silver screen. 'I had nothing to do with that messy business at all. You can snoop about it if you like, Señorita Christie-like, but I have an alibi for Zozobra night. A job. And I tell you – what happened has scared me plenty. I don't scare easily.'

Maddie could well believe that. Both his toughness, and his fear now. They should all be scared. 'Then you know who did this? You think you could be in danger from it, too? You should tell the police!'

Diego laughed wryly. 'The police? I wouldn't talk to them for a million bucks. You think I need *more* trouble?'

'Then tell me,' she whispered.

'You seem like a nice sort. You don't need the trouble, either. I had nothing to do with Ricardo's death, but there's plenty who would be better off with him gone now. Just be careful out there.'

Maddie sensed him and all the things he stored in his brain slipping away. 'Tell me one thing, then! Did you like him at all? Ricardo?'

Diego glanced away. 'Like him? I don't know anyone who *liked* him, really. He had more secrets than most, I would say. He wasn't so bad, though. Unhappy, yeah. He could take out that unhappiness on people around him. But he didn't deserve to end like that.'

He waved to someone, and stood up, straightening the jacket of his fine suit. 'Remember now, Señorita Christie. Be careful, yes?' He smoothed his hair. 'I have to go find employment now.'

Maddie nodded, and watched him vanish into the crowd, all that fear and knowledge concealed behind a charming smile. She drifted back to the bar, where Gunther was chatting with Eva and drinking that fine gin.

'So, what did you discover from the beauteous Diego?' he asked.

'Not a whole lot. He's hard to read. Keeps his cards close.' But even so, she realized he'd told her a lot. Señor Otero and his son, and Juan-Antonio. Ricardo and his secrets and unhappiness.

Gunther nodded gently. 'Oh, darling, a man like that – he has to keep his cards close, you know that. Santa Fe isn't New York, you can do an awful lot here, but it's not a complete paradise. Sometimes none of us can be as completely ourselves as we'd want.'

'I know, darling, I'm sorry. But I really don't think he killed Ricardo, or maybe even know who did it. He says he has an alibi for that night, and it's easy enough to look into that a bit. He definitely knows a lot more than he's saying, though.' Maddie reached for Gunther's glass and took a sip of that delightful gin. 'Did you know Mateo Otero had worries about his son and Juan-Antonio Montoya?'

Gunther's eyes widened in surprise. 'Young Mateo and Juan-Antonio? I hadn't heard even a whisper of such a thing! Mateo might like the boys, true, but not Juan-Antonio. His arguments with his father seemed entirely concerned with art and college and such.'

'I would think so, too. But Señor Otero's suspicions must come from somewhere. I thought it was just a business deal gone sour, but maybe it's more personal.'

'So his worries about his son being led astray are covering for money troubles, or vice versa?'

Maddie sighed. 'I wish I knew. I'll see Señor Otero at a committee meeting at the museum soon, I can have a little chat with him there. In the meantime, Gunther darling, I have a wee favor to ask.'

Gunther looked entirely suspicious. 'Just what sort of favor?'

'Do you need the Duesy tomorrow?'

ELEVEN

D espite the nature of her errand, trying to catch a killer and all that, Maddie couldn't quite contain her burst of joy as the car flew down the winding twists at the top of Canyon Road and then up again, into the foothills. She did love it when Gunther loaned her his car, but that wasn't very often, so she had to take advantage of those moments skimming along the dirt roads. The scarf she'd tied around her hair caught and threatened to blow away, and her gloved hands clutched the steering wheel as she swerved around a pothole. If she returned the darling Duesy damaged, she'd never get her mitts on it again!

It was a glorious day, the sky a cloudless, endless pure pale blue, so close she was sure she could just reach up and grab it. The autumn air had such a crisp, dry bite to it, bringing the green smell of pine, the softness of the season turning.

Sunmount, the TB hospital that drew well-heeled patients from all over the place, was outside of town, built where everyone could take advantage of the fresh air and sunshine, take pleasure in the sublime beauty of the views. David said that one of their ideas was that having a positive outlook on life, allowing the patients to enjoy the peace and loveliness, helped with recovery, and she definitely agreed with him.

She slowed down to turn down the long, paved drive toward the main hospital building. The juniper and piñon trees that lined the track cast purple shadows over the car as she slid down into a shallow valley. It all looked more like a mountain village than a hospital, the main building painted white with its gleaming windows thrown open to the fine weather, its red Spanish-tiled roof glowing. Spread out behind were rows of smaller cottages, each with its own sun porch, and the green plaza for exercise and classes.

She parked on the graveled circle leading to the front doors, and powdered her nose and smoothed her hair. Just because she was on a mission, that didn't mean she couldn't look presentable in case she ran into David! She slid out of the car, giving its hood a fond pat, and made her way up the steps through the carved wood doors.

Inside, it was cool and dim, smelling of fresh air, vases of lavender, and that faint medicinal tang that couldn't be fully escaped. She hurried past the murals on the whitewashed walls, scenes of the mountains and sky, and the curving staircase toward the lobby.

'Mrs Alwin,' the nurse at the front desk said with a welcoming smile. 'Are you here to see Dr Cole? I think he's in consultation right now, but he should be out soon.'

'I wouldn't say no to seeing him!' Maddie answered, straightening her gloves and glancing around the airy, sunny lobby. A few patients in their white linen robes and slippers hurried past toward the billiards room and the lecture hall. 'But I'm also here to visit a patient. A Mr George Marulis?'

'Oh, yes, one of our new ones. He's outside by the exercise ground. One of our restless patients, can't sit still! Are you friends with Mr Marulis?'

'Friend of a friend. I told them I would look in on him, see how he's settling down,' Maddie said, secretly crossing her fingers in her driving gloves. Her old nanny would have gotten the soap out for sure if she knew Maddie was lying! 'I'll just go find him, then.'

She found George Marulis sitting on a bench looking over a group doing their calisthenics on the exercise ground, the cottages stretching behind them. Their white dresses fluttered in the breeze like flowers against the gray-green background of the mountains, the mustard-yellow of the chamisa, and Maddie longed to paint the scene, to capture the colors and feeling of optimism.

But this was time for different work. Detective work.

'Mr Marulis?' she called, marching up to him with her brightest smile painted on her face. 'How do you do. I'm Maddie Alwin.'

He peered up at her. It was hard to imagine him married to

Sofia Montoya, he looked so much older than her, older even than Ricardo and Catalina. His thin face was lined and gray, his eyebrows wild bushes over faded brown eyes. His white robe hung from his bony shoulders, but his arms looked strong enough to stab someone. She couldn't tell at all from that intense gaze whether he was happy or angry to see her.

'I've heard of you. The New York lady artist. Have we met, then?'

'I'm friends with Catalina Montoya. She was a bit worried about you when she heard you were ill. I was coming out here anyway, and told her I would see how you were faring.'

He looked back at the exercise class, almost as if dismissing her. 'She's a decent lady. Unlike her husband.'

Maddie slowly sat down beside him on the bench. The cool breeze caught at her hat and the hem of her blue tweed walking skirt. 'You heard Ricardo Montoya passed away?'

George snorted. 'Was hacked up and tossed away, you mean! Everyone's heard about *that*. Not the way I would have expected him to go, but I can't weep over it. I feel for Catalina and her children, though, I certainly do.'

Maddie nodded, thinking of the rumor she'd heard that he might marry Sofia. 'You, um, didn't get along with him, then?'

'He wasn't the worst man I ever came across in my business dealings, but he wasn't as shrewd as he wanted everyone to think. He gave me some bad advice. Very bad advice.'

'Did he, indeed? I'm glad I never invested with him, then.'

'Others in this town weren't so lucky, Mrs Alwin, I can tell you that. He would have bounced back, he always did. So will they, now that he's gone.' He looked back at the hospital, the red-tile roof gleaming in the autumn light, a thoughtful frown on his brow. 'I won't have that chance, not for a long time.'

'The doctors and treatment here are excellent, Mr Marulis! I'm sure you'll be quite well, and back to your business here in Santa Fe in no time.'

'Once I'm out of Sunmount, I'm leaving Santa Fe. Not much left for me here now.' That frown turned to a full-blown scowl.

'I did hear you were possibly going to marry Sofia Montoya.'

He glanced down at her, and she thought for a moment he

would burst into laughter. He just scowled again. 'And where did you hear that?'

'Oh – gossip. Here and there. You know how it is around town.'

'Another reason to leave. Always that infernal gossip. Ricardo once suggested I might marry Sofia, that's true. A business arrangement of sorts, though she's a pretty girl. I never married, and it's high time I did, so everyone says. Nothing official, though, and you can tell that to your gossips.' He turned back to her, his expression full of suspicion. 'Catalina didn't send you to try and push through an engagement, did she?'

'Not at all. I think she's contemplating different arrangements for her family, now that she's a widow.' Maddie thought of Sofia dancing blissfully with her young Jake, and doubted any power at all could turn her away now. 'In fact, I imagine Sofia will soon be married to someone else. Someone her father probably wouldn't have approved of.'

George gave a bark of laughter. 'Good for her! I hope that whole family will do shocking things now. Do them good after so long with Ricardo. Liked getting his own way, he did. I just wish I could have done the same, before it was too late.'

'Were you friends with Ricardo very long? Before you went into business together, maybe. My father always said you shouldn't mix real friendship with business.' Then again, much like Ricardo, her father never seemed the sort to have *real* friends. Only people who came to his dinners and dances to do those business deals.

The more Maddie looked at Ricardo Montoya, the more he puzzled her. He seemed to have so many contradictions, so many secrets, despite the public sort of life he led.

'I suppose we were, once. We were at school at St Michael's together as boys. He was a wonderful tennis player, I remember, while I was an awkward lad with my nose in books. Some of the boys teased me because of that, but not Ricardo. He helped me improve my backhand tremendously so I could actually win a match here and there. I had forgotten about that. We lost touch when he went away to university, though, and I took over my father's work. Only saw each other at Fiesta.

Until he had this business idea . . .' George frowned into the distance, as if he saw long-gone days rather than the exercise green.

'It sounds like he was very different as a young man,' Maddie said. Masks and fears, they were always there. Just like Fiesta parties.

'We all have things we'd rather people didn't see. Don't you think so, Mrs Alwin?'

'Certainly I do. When was the last time you saw him?'

'A few weeks ago, at a Fiesta meeting of the *cofradia*. He was quiet, distracted. Wouldn't talk to any of us about business. I wasn't able to do much after that.'

'I suppose you haven't been feeling well.'

'I feel fine!' he snapped. 'Just coughing up a tiny bit of blood, my worry-wart housekeeper made me go to the doctor. Always fussing, she is. Been with me too long.'

'You're bally well lucky she did! Now you have a better chance of recovery, don't you?'

He chuckled. 'Right you are, Mrs Alwin. We should all have *someone* to look after us.'

'Have you been here at Sunmount long, then?' she asked, though she knew he was rather new there. That he could have had time to commit the murder before he went into the hospital.

'A couple of days, maybe. Who knows? Time's all the same in places like this. Maybe less.'

'Mr Marulis!' a nurse called as she hurried up the pathway toward them, her dark blue cape fluttering in the wind. 'It's time for your lunch. You need to eat plenty of good food, you know!'

George pushed himself to his feet. He seemed more wistful, nostalgic maybe, than angry now. 'Well, Mrs Alwin, thank you for coming here, though I'm not sure why you did. It was good to remember for a bit, we shouldn't hold on to bitterness toward the dead. Give my condolences to Catalina. And my congratulations to Sofia.'

'I will,' Maddie said, and realized she had to finish her talking quickly now. 'Oh, Mr Marulis – was anyone else, anyone specific you knew of, hit hard by Ricardo's business dealings?'

'Ha! Just about everyone with any extra coin to invest in Santa Fe, I'd say. Fernandez, one of the Seligman brothers, the Luhans. Any number of 'em. Glad you didn't put in any money, Mrs Alwin!' He walked away with the nurse, leaving Maddie to slowly stroll along the winding pathways, past a croquet ground, a net for badminton. She went over what she'd learned, that George Marulis and Ricardo Montoya had once been good friends and George now felt betrayed. That several people in town had lost from that business deal, including Señor Fernandez.

As she came to the top of the wide graveled path that led back to the main hospital building, she glimpsed the very welcome sight of David hurrying toward her, tall and strong in his white coat, his hair like autumn gold. She waved and rushed to meet him, kissing him on the cheek before he took her hand and they turned toward the hospital building.

'How was our new patient Mr Marulis, then?' he asked.

'A bit gruff at first, but then he was an utter lamb.'

'Of course. He was talking to *you*, how could he help but melt?'

'I think that only works on *you*, darling. He did lose a packet on some business venture of Ricardo's, but they were once boyhood friends. I have the feeling he *could* kill someone in the heat of anger, he's a moody so-and-so. Do you think he would be strong enough?'

David thought this over for a moment. 'To do the murder, yes. I'm not sure he could have dumped the body in an arroyo, though. I suppose he could have had an accomplice.'

'He also said a lot of other people lost on that scheme, so someone *could* have helped him. I'll have to ask around a bit more, make a list. In the meantime, did I hear there was lunch? One of the nurses thought I was meeting you. I'm absolutely gasping for a cup of tea, and I have to be at the art museum for a last committee meeting about that masquerade ball. You'll come with me, won't you? To the ball?'

'Of course I will! It's a chance for a dance, and . . .' His expression suddenly shifted to one of horror. 'I won't have to wear a costume, will I?'

Maddie laughed, and squeezed his hand. 'You certainly will.

It's a *masquerade* ball. I think Juanita has the costumes in hand, so don't worry – she would never embarrass you too greatly.'

'Couldn't I get away with a mask and my evening suit?'

'Don't be a party-pooper. You've seen how everyone here loves an elaborate costume.' Circus parties, teddy bear picnics, flamenco themes, 'Old Vienna', she'd been to them all. Mostly organized by Will Shuster. 'I suppose I could use the committee meeting to find out more opinions about Ricardo. They've all known each other so long.'

'What about Señor Fernandez?'

'He's definitely in love with Catalina, and I would guess probably has been for a long time.' Maddie thought of how André and Catalina looked together, laughing and easy and comfortable. And it sounded like Fernandez had lost some money in Ricardo's scheme on top of all that. 'We should take a closer peek at him. For now, though, I want my lunch!'

TWELVE

Maddie hurried up the front steps of the Museum of Art, running a wee bit late for her committee meeting. But she couldn't help but pause at the doors, smiling as she looked around the building that was almost like a second home to her. The interior, like the tower-bedecked exterior, was made to look old, even though it was only a few years finished, with cool stone floors, a shady courtyard, and tan-tinted walls that held a colorful array of paintings.

She waved at her friend Olive Rush, her red turban askew as she perched on a ladder to straighten one of the light fixtures. In one of the small side galleries, she glimpsed Paul Vynne, studying a Berninghaus painting of swirling pinks and yellows with a solemn look on his face. She called out to him, and he turned with a wave.

'Mrs Alwin!' Paul said, a wide smile breaking over his serious expression. 'How lovely to see you again.'

'And you, Mr Vynne. Are you quite all right after our Zozobra night?'

He laughed ruefully, and rubbed his hand over his stubbled jaw. Maddie saw he really was a handsome man, with bright green eyes and a rugged, slightly messy, very artistic aura about him. But he looked tired, the lines around his eyes deeper. 'I'd say so. It sounds like the real shock came after. Will is always saying how peaceful it is here, a quiet place to get some work done, but now I'm not so sure I believe him.'

'It usually is, I promise. Are you here alone? Escaping from the chaos at Will's place?'

'It *is* lively, isn't it? But then, he always was full of energy, even when we were young. I'm here with an old art teacher of mine, Herr Rotheim, who moved to Albuquerque a few

years ago. He brought along a prospective student.' He glanced
past Maddie's shoulder, and waved. 'There they are now!'

Maddie turned to see an older gentleman, with silver hair
and small mustache, his dark eyes magnified by a pince-nez,
a well-cut gray coat draped over his shoulders. She thought
she recognized him from the photos in Paul's casita. With him
was Juan-Antonio Montoya.

'Maddie, this is my old teacher, Herr Rotheim, a great
genius!' Paul said. 'And I think you know Juan-Antonio
Montoya? This is Madeline Alwin, a Santa Fe artist.'

'Ah, Madame Alwin, I have heard of you,' Herr Rotheim
said with a courtly bow. 'I am pleased to make your acquaintance at last. I fear I do not often make it to Santa Fe these
days.'

'And I'm very pleased to meet you,' Maddie said.

'You're friends with my mother, aren't you?' Juan-Antonio
said. 'How's her portrait coming along? I'd love to see it, hear
any painting tips you might have. Portraiture isn't my strong
spot, but I want to improve.'

'But I've heard you're very good,' Maddie said. 'So much
potential.'

To her surprise, Juan-Antonio blushed a bit, looking like the
very young man he really was, and he shuffled his well-shod
feet on the wooden planks of the floor. 'I hope to be someday,
I really do. Soon. I love it so much, art. And now I can . . .'

Now he was free to pursue it, with his father's expectations
thrown off? Maddie could understand that, understand the wild
compulsion to create and how it felt when that impulse was
stifled, suffocated under convention. Juan-Antonio had looked
angry enough before. But it was hard to reconcile this young
man, his cheeks pink with eagerness, with the need to create
and not destroy, with cold-blooded patricide and body chopper-
upper. He held out a small sketchbook and showed her a scene
of a church on a hillside, a gathering of people in its courtyard.
There was something familiar about the line of the clouds, the
sense of movement, but she couldn't quite grasp it.

'Now he'll have some proper instruction, too,' Paul said
with a kind smile for Juan-Antonio. 'I asked Herr Rotheim if
he was taking new pupils.'

'I said yes, certainly, when I saw Mr Montoya's portfolio,' Herr Rotheim said. 'I trust Paul's artistic judgment implicitly, and he was quite right about this young man's promise. He just needs a stronger grounding in technique, a chance to find his own style. The instinct is there. You know how it is, Mrs Alwin, if you are an artist yourself.'

'Yes, indeed,' Maddie agreed. Finding her own 'voice' on canvas had been the hardest thing, and surely Juan-Antonio, just as she herself had been growing up, was told to have no voice at all.

Juan-Antonio's expression hardened a bit as he glanced at the painting on the wall behind them, a scene of a pueblo dance, all bright colors and swirling movement. 'I was never allowed proper lessons before. I'm so far behind where I should be.'

'Not at all!' Herr Rotheim said. 'A year or so of hard work, you will be much improved. *Hard* work, you understand.'

'Oh, yes, I will!' Juan-Antonio declared. 'Day and night, Herr Rotheim.'

'Will you leave Santa Fe, then?' Maddie asked. She'd be able to give Catalina a good report of her son's abilities, but also the news that she'd lose him to 'day and night' painting.

'Just to go to Albuquerque for a time, for Herr Rotheim's school. Then Paul offered to help me find a course back East when I'm done, to polish things up, make some contacts.' Herr Rotheim called Juan-Antonio's attention to a painting, and he smiled as he excused himself. 'But I'll see you at the funeral, won't I, Mrs Alwin? My mother said you'd be there.'

'Yes, of course.' Maddie glanced at Paul as the young man hurried away, wondering why he went so out of his way for a young artist he'd just met. 'That was very kind of you, to look out for him.'

'I always like to help out young artists when I can, as I was once helped by so many people,' Paul answered. 'And I feel for Juan-Antonio, losing his dad like that. But I understand *you* have a painting here in the museum. I'd love to see it.'

'Yes, it's just in that gallery over there! I do love to show it off, I admit.' She led him toward the next room, where her garden scene hung. She saw Juan-Antonio and Herr Rotheim up ahead, their heads closely bent over a small watercolor. Juan-Antonio did look so excited about art. 'Will you stay much longer in Santa Fe?'

'Not much longer, no. In fact, I hope to leave in the next day or two, now that I've seen Will again. Just long enough to make sure Juan-Antonio there is settled.'

'Living with Will has driven you off, then?'

He laughed. 'Not at all. It's easy to be rid of Will's chatter when you need to, just say you have to be painting. Art is sacred for him. And he's been so busy with your Fiesta.'

'That's why I'm here, actually. A committee meeting for a Fiesta masquerade ball, I offered to advise on their artistic backdrops.'

'We shouldn't make you late, then!'

'I always have time to explore the museum.' She waved at a large painting of a man wrapped in a bright blanket, staring with palpable longing at a cloudy sky. 'Have you been able to get any work done while you're here?'

'Some, yes. Enough to make a mess of Will's casita. I can't keep away from a paintbrush very long.' He paused next to a large dark canvas. A woman in a black gown and cobweb-like lace veil stared out at the viewer with huge gray eyes, one hand held out toward a river that flowed behind her, moonlight touching the water with gold. 'This looks fearsome. Is she a witch?'

Maddie studied the scene, and remembered the twins demanding to know she 'wasn't real'. 'A water spirit, I would say, or something like that. She is La Llorona. A bit of a Medea figure, her husband betrayed her and she tossed her children into the river. She regretted it immediately, of course, and now she haunts the water, crying for her lost babies. I've been reading a book about her with my housekeeper's daughters, I think she's hoping it will keep them out of the arroyos at flash-flood time.'

'Arroyos?'

'Ditches that keep the flood waters away from houses in the spring.'

'Were those the girls I saw you with at the parade? Little princesses in a castle-wagon?' he asked.

'You saw us there?' Maddie said, and remembered glimpsing Paul across the plaza.

'I would have come by to talk, but the crowd was so thick.'

'It always is at the Fiesta parades! And everyone does love their pets and kids. The girls won a prize that day, it was very exciting.'

'It was a great spectacle. No La Llorona there that I could see to mess it up!'

'She only comes out at night.'

'Sounds like it can be dangerous for children around here,' Paul said. 'Flood ditches and water spirits . . .'

'And murders?' Maddie shivered. 'It's usually not. Santa Fe is such a small place, really, everyone knows each other's children and where they belong. I guess I do worry, though. They're like my own in so many ways, and I just want the world to be lovely and peaceful for them.'

'They're lucky to have you. To have so many people watching out for them,' Paul said wistfully. 'No kids of your own?'

'My husband died not too long after we married. What about you?'

'No, not for me. Never married at all. It's good for my strange working hours, but just – lonely sometimes, I guess.'

'You do seem to have lots of friends, though, like Will and Herr Rotheim.'

'Sure, I have friends, other artists, all over the world! Even old school friends, though not so many of them now.' He looked sad for a moment, very far away, until he smiled at her. 'I'm afraid I'm keeping you from your meeting. It was very nice to see you again. I'm so glad to hear Will has such fine friends here. He is very lucky indeed.'

He excused himself to examine a painting on the far wall, and Maddie realized it was nearly time for her meeting. She gathered up her portfolio of sketches for the masquerade ball designs and made her way to the studios just beyond the courtyard set aside for the meeting. She hated having to go inside, the courtyard was blooming with early autumn color, the last of the summer blossoms, and people were gathered to sketch and chat under the four sides of the shaded portal.

The new murals Will had worked on shimmered with color, red and blues and pure whites.

But she left it behind to step into the studio, the windows shaded, tables laid out and spread with drawings. A few people were already there, sipping tea from the bronze urn Olive brought out for such occasions, and Maddie glimpsed Mateo Otero at the back of the room, alone for the moment as he stared between the shades to the street below. She remembered what Diego said about him, that he thought his son was being led astray by Juan-Antonio, as well as the financial troubles. It seemed like a good time for a little chat with him.

'Señor Otero,' she said as she came to his side, looking down at the same window view. People were streaming past toward the Fiesta booths on the plaza, all movement and laughter in contrast to Señor Otero's silent solemnity. Car horns honked for mules and horses to get out of the way, and children shrieked at a puppet show. 'How is your wife? I had heard she once was on this committee, I'm surprised not to see her today.'

He shivered, as if stirring himself to talk but he didn't look at her. 'She has gone to Albuquerque with our son. We are thinking of sending him to a boarding school there before he goes to university next year,' he said quietly. 'But this ball is an important tradition, we knew one of us had to be here to make certain the finishing touches are correct.'

'Oh, yes. I think the balcony decorations will be splendid, and the bower where the orchestra will play. I have some ideas . . .' She started to open her portfolio, but he waved it away. 'And we must be brave to go ahead, as I'm sure Señor Montoya would have wished. After such an awful thing to happen.'

Señor Otero frowned. 'As he would have wished?'

'I know the Montoyas were very involved in the life of the town. The church, charities, balls like this one . . .'

'Hmph. So he wanted everyone to think. But yes, the Montoyas once did much for Santa Fe, in the old times, I suppose.' His expression suddenly shifted, as if he realized he'd spoken too much. 'But yes, you are quite right, Mrs Alwin. We should make this ball a tribute.'

'What a fine idea. Will your wife and son be there? I am

sure Juan-Antonio and Sofia would like to see young people, if they are able to attend in their mourning.'

His fist clenched on the windowsill. 'My son and Juan-Antonio are not friendly.'

Maddie clucked sympathetically. 'I do understand. After the business troubles . . .'

'When that real-estate scheme failed, it is true I no longer had trust in Ricardo's judgment. Many of us suffered for that, and I would not have taken his advice again. But business is just that, Mrs Alwin – business. As I'm sure you understand. Family is something else entirely, and sometimes things, once known, can never be unknown.' He turned on his heel abruptly and walked away, seating himself at the far end of the table, leaving Maddie uncertain.

Maria Gutierrez, Catalina's old friend, came to her side and handed her a cup of tea. Her fringed shawl and feathered hat trembled. 'Don't worry about Mateo. I have known him a very long time. He can be such an old bear sometimes. He has been forever, so his wife always says.'

'He says we should make the ball a tribute to Ricardo Montoya.'

Señora Gutierrez looked surprised. 'Did he, indeed? Well – excellent idea. Did Mateo really think of it?'

'Yes. Is he not usually thoughtful in such ways?'

'He always does what's proper, of course. But they were not the greatest of friends, as I'm afraid you've seen.'

'Yes,' Maddie mused. She had seen that. Was it the real-estate deal gone sour – or the two families' sons?

'You must not mind us,' Maria said with a strained little laugh. 'We have all known each other an age, and have our little arguments and disagreements! I should never like you to have the wrong idea of us, Mrs Alwin.'

'I would not dream of it, Señora Gutierrez.'

Maddie decided to make a detour on the walk home to the little park tucked beside the cathedral, behind the hospital where she often went with David on his short breaks. Through those wrought-iron gates, it all seemed peaceful, with beds of pink and red and white flowers wound round with paths, green-painted benches, a fountain humming. Birds splashed there, bits of blue and white, and children laughed as they rolled along their hoops. The hum of the Fiesta on the plaza, just a few blocks away, was muted there, the light gleaming honey-amber on the square stone bell towers.

She loved to stroll those gravel pathways, studying the way the sunlight filtered through the old trees, the nodding blossoms in the breeze casting out their heavenly perfume. The trees and shrubs were just changing at their tips, to their autumn garb of yellow and sandy-red. It was all such an inspiration for her work, a moment to be outside of herself and part of the larger world, the sky and trees and light. It was why she'd made her home, there, after all, to be surrounded by beauty and nature and freedom.

She frowned as she thought of the meeting, of Señor Otero and Maria Gutierrez, of all the hidden parts of life here. Secrets so old they just seemed part of the scenery now. Until they burst out into violence.

It was too much like New York, like her family and their friends, and all the things hidden in silence.

'Maddie! I'm surprised to see you here. I would have thought you'd be busy with all the Fiesta doings,' someone called, and Maddie turned to see her friend Father Malone hurrying toward her, his rotund black cassock-draped figure and twinkling eyes behind his spectacles a welcome sight.

'Father Malone! How lovely to see you again,' Maddie said, meeting him under one of the old trees. 'Juanita told me *you* have been busy lately. Weddings and christenings and a new choir!'

'Oh, yes. My choir is shaping up quite spic and span lately, I must say, with the extra rehearsals. They'll be in splendid form for the archbishop's novena.' He offered her his arm, and they strolled past the fountain, dodging a hoop. 'But right now I've just come from Catalina Montoya's house. The authorities have said we can go ahead with the funeral, and she wanted to make plans for the Mass.'

'How is she today? We've rather become friends since I've been working on her portrait.'

'She said you've been a great help to her. She seemed well

enough, I would say. A bit tired, of course. I think she took a bit of comfort in making plans. She's always been a great supporter of the cathedral, heading our altar flowers committee, raising funds for the new bells.' He glanced down at her, his eyes glinting behind his spectacles. 'Perhaps you've been of *help* taking a closer look at what happened to poor Ricardo? As at the film set.'

Maddie laughed wryly. 'You do know me now. It all seemed so very bizarre, and Inspector Sadler doesn't seem to have gotten terribly far. I thought I'd just ask a few questions around town, see what I can find.'

'And have you found very much?'

She sighed. 'A lot more confusion! What do you think of it all? Ricardo seemed to be someone everyone knew, yet the people I've spoken to all seem to have varied views of him. He hardly seems like one man at all.'

Father Malone shook his head, his round face serious beneath his broad-brimmed black hat. 'It is true that we don't always know people as well as we think we do. I know so many people like the Montoyas from my work here. Powerful old families, sometimes. You should be careful. People don't always like their secrets poked at, you know, my dear.'

'And don't I know it! You aren't the first to warn me I should be careful, Father.' Diego, Señora Gutierrez. 'Why is that?'

'Well, I worry about you. Where would I borrow my detective novels, if you weren't here in Santa Fe?' He patted her hand with a reassuring smile. 'I know you aren't foolish, Maddie. There is just so much you and I can't really see, being from far away. It might help us view things a bit more clearly sometimes, as we don't know all the old stories, the old relationships. But it also means we're always viewed with a bit of suspicion. If we want to live here, to be trusted . . .'

'Yes, I know. You are quite right. And I do want to stay here, so very much. I don't want enemies.'

'I can say that it's true Ricardo Montoya had lost some of that trust in recent times, through missteps and wrong turns. I don't know all the details, but he had started to make misjudgments in business dealings, which was not like him before.

And his marriage and friendships – they weren't on the steadiest of grounds. Between us.'

Maddie nodded. She knew he would give her no details, not if he gained knowledge from the confessional. 'Between us. I can see what you mean.'

The bells tolled the hour, and he took his leave of her to make it to his next appointment. Maddie urged him to come to dinner soon, to borrow two or three new books, and waved him off.

She turned toward the police station once she left the gates. Mentioning Inspector Sadler made her realize she hadn't seen him in a while, and wondered what he might have found. Not that he would tell her much, of course, not willingly, but she could see what little details she might winkle out.

It turned out she didn't have to go as far as the station. She glimpsed his battered bowler hat on the street corner across from La Fonda. He studied the bustling plaza, where a dance orchestra played on the bandstand and young couples shyly waltzed in the shade. He was munching on a bag of popcorn, crumbs caught in his mustache.

He gave her an amusingly guilty glance when he saw her watching, and swiped some of the crumbs away.

'Mrs Alwin,' he said. 'Just patrolling the Fiesta, making sure all is peaceful.'

'So I see,' Maddie said, trying not to giggle. 'Making sure the food is up to standards?'

'You won't tell Mrs Sadler? I'm really supposed to be on, well, on some terrible diet thing,' he whispered.

Maddie was shocked. 'There is a Mrs Sadler?'

'Yes. For thirty years. She doesn't get out much, too shy. But she does like to watch like a hawk over her house. And me.'

'Indeed?' Maddie longed to meet the woman who could stand to keep a hawklike watch on Sadler. She must be formidable. 'And she has put you on a diet?'

'For my health, the doctor says.' He patted at the belly straining his black waistcoat. 'I'm fit as a fiddle, though, and I keep telling the missus!'

'Of course you are, Inspector.' Maddie studied the crowd swirling past, the blur of the children circling on the Tio Vivo carousel, the dancers. 'And has all been peaceful lately, under your watch?'

'Today, sure. Had to throw a couple of drunks into jail last night, though, for fistfights.'

'No more body parts, though.'

He scowled. 'Not yet. And I *sure* don't want to find you in a firepit next, Mrs Alwin, so watch where you step, eh?'

Maddie shivered at the thought of being the next victim like that. At least she knew there were people watching out for her, warning her. 'Everyone keeps telling me to be careful, but I promise I always am! I have lots of painting to do before I'm done here, Inspector, and I don't intend to hop off the planet early.'

'But you've been snooping a bit, I'm sure,' he said sourly.

'Not snooping. Just – observing. It seems Ricardo Montoya was not the most popular man in town lately.'

'That real-estate thing? Yeah, there are a few who are sore about that. Makes me glad I'm not an investing man. No gambling. Money in the drawer, savings, that's what we all need.'

Maddie thought of her own family in New York, her father and brother and the way they pored over the financial news-papers. She rather agreed with Sadler, especially if Ricardo had been losing his friends' money lately. Her own inheritance was safely tucked away in conservative investments, luckily. 'Very sensible of you.' She felt a bit sorry for him, dieting and all, so she told him a bit more of what she'd found lately, the Montoyas' family quarrels. She concealed a few things, though, like the visit to the Golden Rooster.

By the time they parted, and Maddie glimpsed the inspector stopping at the caramel apple booth, she feared she was no closer to a clear view at all.

THIRTEEN

'Let perpetual light shine upon them, and help us so to believe where we have not seen . . .'

Maddie bowed her head as she listened to Father Malone lead Ricardo's funeral Mass at the altar of the cathedral, his mourning vestments somber against the brightly painted panels of saints and angels, the light streaming from the stained-glass windows. It wasn't as full as the funeral of a man like a Montoya would usually be; perhaps people were scared off by the macabre manner of his death, or his business actions in life. But the pews nearest the altar were crowded enough. Catalina sat there, her face covered by a black lace-edged veil, her gloved hands held on either side by her children. Juan-Antonio seemed distracted, while Sofia sniffled into her handkerchief.

André Fernandez sat behind them, close to Catalina, and Diego and Mrs Hurst, as well as Juanita's cousin Priscilla, were across the aisle. Mrs Hurst tapped her toe, while Diego seemed to be holding back a little smile. His suit was sure spiffy, Maddie thought, beautifully tailored and of a fine fabric.

Maddie turned ahead to the altar, and took a deep breath to steady herself. Funerals were always so difficult. They sent her straight back to that gray, rainy day at Grace Church, Pete's funeral without a coffin. He'd been lost in the mud of France. The scent of lilies, overpoweringly sweet, the tang of incense from the swinging censer, the hum of a choir. She swayed a bit, and David squeezed her hand.

She glanced at him, at his worried face, and flashed him a quick smile. She held on to him, and studied the church around them to remind herself she was far away from *that* day. It was a very pretty church, French Gothic, not terribly old, all sunny, airy vaulted ceilings and gilded pillars. She often liked to duck inside to absorb the cool, calm hush of it all, to share Chesterton novels with Father Malone. Even today, with the good Father looking so solemn in his black and purple, the muffled sobs, the dolorous music, she found the light helped hold her still.

She turned the page of her prayer book, and studied the gathering from under the brim of her black velvet hat. Rickie, the young constable, was there, keeping an eye on everything. She recognized a few people from the committee meetings, even some who had been angry about Ricardo's faulty business advice. The Baumanns and Shusters represented the artists, and even Will seemed subdued. But no one jumped up and shouted, 'It was me! I did it!' and there were no black-veiled mystery women crying at the back of the church.

A wave of organ music washed over them, and at last Father Malone said, 'Here in this last act, in sorrow but without fear, in love and appreciation, we commit Ricardo Juan Sebastian Montoya's soul to its natural end. Amen.'

But of course it was *not* a natural end. Maddie couldn't help remember seeing him there in that arroyo as she watched the mourners process slowly up the aisle, its tiled floor muffled in a purple carpet. Perhaps someone in that group had even caused that *un*natural end.

Will and Nancy came at the end of the line, and Maddie and David joined them as they moved through the heavy bronze doors into the real world again. The daylight, even though it was a bit overcast, made her blink hard after the diffuse, stained-glass glow. They could still hear the music from the Fiesta, just a little way away on the plaza, and it seemed so odd.

'Maddie,' Father Malone said with a kind smile. 'Will you be joining us for a reception at the refectory? The committal will be later, at Rosario Cemetery, but Mrs Montoya wanted a small gathering. She tells me you've been very helpful to her lately.'

'Oh, yes, of course.' Maddie glanced at Catalina, who stood at the center of a small group near the serene St Francis statue. André stood near her, as Sofia whispered with her Jake and Juan-Antonio was nowhere to be seen. 'It must be so difficult for her, with everything uncertain.'

'She is fortunate in her friends. And of course we here at the church will do whatever we can for her.' After he greeted a few straggling mourners, he asked after her latest read, and the twins' schooling, before promising to come to dinner very soon. David offered Maddie his arm, and she slid her gloved fingers around his elbow, glad of his steady warmth. The day seemed so chilly, even though it actually had a warm autumn tang to the air.

'Shall we?' he said.

'Are you sure you have the time for the reception?' she asked. 'You're usually out at Sunmount today.'

'Dr McKee is taking over for me. I couldn't leave you alone like this. Funerals are always so hard.'

Maddie leaned her head on his shoulder, feeling lighter knowing she was not really alone. Not any more. 'You are a darling.'

He kissed her forehead quickly, and studied the milling gathering in the church forecourt. 'So – do you have any ideas about what really happened?'

'Now, why would I have *ideas*?'

He laughed gently. 'When it comes to trouble, you always have ideas.'

Maddie had to sigh in agreement. 'I just can't help it, I guess. All those Christie novels I read. I do hate seeing a mess for someone as nice as Catalina to worry over! The problem is, I have too many ideas and none quite fit together. Ricardo Montoya was such a puzzle.'

'Most people are complicated like that. Contrary.'

'Very true. But it does make it really hard to see which *complication* got him killed!'

Catalina excused herself from her friends, and came up to Maddie to smile and kiss her cheek. She smelled of violet powder and Jicky, so Maddie knew where Sofia got it. 'You will join us, won't you, Maddie? And you, Dr Cole. It's just a small reception, but I would love to have you there, you've been so kind to me at this terrible time.'

'Yes, certainly, Catalina. We're honored you invited us,' Maddie answered. André called Catalina away, and Maddie held on to David's hand as they went down the steps to the street. The music from the plaza seemed louder there, life moving ahead at full speed no matter what happened mere feet away.

'You will be careful, won't you, Maddie?' David said quietly, seriously.

'I'm always careful!'

He snorted, and she laughed to remember the times she was not nearly as 'careful' as she should have been, like at the movie set. 'Indeed. But Ricardo Montoya's murder was so full of rage. I would hate to see you caught in that, you know. More than hate it.'

She squeezed his arm, and thought of his late wife, the way he lost her. 'You are the sweetest to worry about me. And believe me, I don't want to end up in trouble, either! It did seem terribly, well, personal, didn't it?'

'Personal?'

'Ricardo's murder. Like someone was furious with *him*.'

'I doubt it was a passing maniac, or a robbery gone wrong. Why wouldn't they take his watch? It does feel like this was just a specific act on a specific person. But if whoever did it thought *you* had suspicions . . .'

Maddie nodded. People would go far for self-protection. 'I won't be foolish, I promise. Or I promise I will at least *try* not to be a silly-billy.'

'Because I could never bear it if something happened to you.'

She looked up at him, at those glorious blue eyes, that face that had become so dear to her. 'I couldn't bear it if something happened to you, either. So stick close to me!'

'Now that is a promise I can easily make.'

They held hands as they made their way to the end of the street, to the refectory of the Christian Brothers, who had run Ricardo's old school at St Michael's. It wasn't a grand or fancy place, but comfortable with its whitewashed walls and scrubbed tables, the art on the walls, saints and angels and cherubs, and an array of refreshments and drinks. A string quartet played, the music gentle and soothing as everyone gathered in small knots and groups to chat.

David was drawn aside by one of his patients who longed

to complain about her foot corns, and Maddie took a cup of fruit punch and drifted away to study some of the art, not wanting at all to hear about someone's toes. One of the images was a very fine copy of a Velázquez only with the cathedral itself added into the scene, a cloudy sky as a backdrop to a saint's revelation, all movement and emotion. The style seemed rather familiar.

She remembered that Sister Mary Cecilia mentioned Juan-Antonio had a painting displayed in that room, one he did at school, and she examined this scene for anything like the sketches he'd shown her at the museum. She saw tiny initials in the corner, JM.

What *was* that familiar feeling about it, though? She puzzled over the brushstrokes, the use of color, and at last the memory clicked together. The 'Velázquez' on the wall of the Montoya house. The clouds had just that same distinctive effect, and the line of the robes of the saint, swooping in an imagined wind. But that 'Velázquez' had been made to look old, with a sepia craquelure, and this one did not. Why would Juan-Antonio do that?

Was he involved in some sort of art forgery scheme after all? Was he trying to fool his own parents – or was it all at the behest of his father, another business scheme? And if Ricardo had not known when he hung that painting on his wall, what happened when he found out?

She glanced over at Juan-Antonio, startled by that dawning suspicion. It did seem far-fetched, but then again so was finding bits of a man in Zozobra. She thought of the museum, the sketches he'd shown her, his happiness at finding an art teacher. Making his own choices.

Juan-Antonio noticed her watching him, and hurried over to hand her a fresh glass of punch. He looked curious, but not guilty or furtive or angry.

'Thank you,' she said. 'This is your work? Sister Mary Cecilia said you did have one displayed here, that everyone at school thought you were talented. I see they were right.'

'Yes.' He cast a frowning, critical study over it. 'I should have done this bit of sky so differently. It doesn't have the emotion I wanted, the intensity.'

'That will come with practice. I do like the way you did the saint's robes, and these shadows here. Herr Rotheim is lucky to have you as a pupil.'

His cheeks reddened. He would learn to take compliments with practice, too, she was sure. 'I'm the lucky one, to be finally working on what I want. Finding my way in life.'

'So no Harvard?'

He scowled. 'That was all my father's idea. Now, with Mr Vynne's help, I have a different path.'

'But your father did display some of your work.'

Juan-Antonio gave her a puzzled glance. 'Did he? He wouldn't.'

'Your Velázquez copy. In the upstairs corridor.'

He laughed. 'Oh. Yes. Not too bad, is it? I was reading a book on antique methods and gave it a try.'

'Not bad at all. I was nearly fooled.' She turned to face him. 'Did your father not know it was yours?'

'My mother hung it there, said she'd found it in a market years ago.' He laughed a little louder, catching a few glances and glares. 'Papa didn't know a Velázquez from the swimming pool, he liked to brag about it. I just took a bit of satisfaction that he took pleasure in something he disdained for me.'

'I can understand that. I would have loved to have fooled my parents.' She studied the painting again, and wondered if he was telling her the truth. He did seem too guileless, so wrapped up in his world of art, but was it an act? 'I know you and your father did not often see eye to eye.'

'I'd say so. He didn't understand me at all, he never did. We quarreled so much. Even to the end.'

'Did you see him the day he died?'

Juan-Antonio scuffed his toe along the floor. 'No. I was at the museum that day, then went to a party. Or maybe two or three parties. There was Poquaque Lightning, I don't remember much for a while. If I had known what would happen – if I had just . . .' He kicked his foot harder.

Maddie patted his arm. She didn't want to suspect him; he didn't seem like a hardened art forger. But then, as David said, people were contrary. Complicated. Being held back from a life a person was sure they were meant to have would be painful.

'You couldn't have done anything,' she murmured. But now surely *she* could. There had to be something that would make it all click into place.

FOURTEEN

Maddie went to her studio after Juanita's tea and biscochitos the day after the funeral, to try and get more work done on Catalina's portrait before a last fitting of her costume for the ball. As she buttoned her work smock, she studied the way the light fell on the half-finished brushstrokes, the sea-green in the folds of Catalina's gown and the hint of ultramarine in the dark hair. She would need more mauveine for that.

The sketches she'd made would help deepen the expression, too, give it that spark that could make a portrait truly speak of that person. Make it truly *them* and no one else. As Juan-Antonio had to learn to do.

She sighed as she laid out the sketches on a table, and wished she could use her artistic training to look under the masks of everyone around her and see what secrets they hid around Ricardo's death. She feared she'd never had a class in that sort of thing before! Only anatomy.

Maybe Juan-Antonio would find that knack of looking deeper when he went to art school, as she'd never been able to do. It was so important, both for art *and* life. He did seem passionate about painting, about learning all he could. She'd recognized so well that glow in his eyes at the museum, for she'd once had it herself. She'd also felt that elation of suddenly being freed to run after her dreams, the bonds of her family and New York society slipping away so she could snatch up a sketchbook.

Juan-Antonio was free now, too, as his sister and Catalina were, and they all seemed relieved, happy even, about that. Maddie examined the background in Catalina's sketches, the black and white pencil lines of the extravagant Montoya house.

Mr Marulis said Ricardo wasn't really a bad person, or once he was not. It seemed to Maddie he was just someone who needed to maintain control at all times, to always make sure others saw him only as he wished to be seen. She understood that impulse; it was there in her own parents. And just like with Ricardo's family, it drove away those who should love each other the most. But what was Ricardo so desperate to control? His finances? His romantic life? His family? Had it all burst out suddenly and led to his death?

She took out a scrap of paper, and started to write down what she knew so far, which sadly wasn't much.

There was the family, of course. Catalina, who seemed so much younger and lighter now, so happy to move on with her old friend André Fernandez, who also seemed to have waited a long time for Catalina. Could they have conspired to do away with Ricardo, to have their love and also their respectability in their home town and families? Agatha Christie so often said people would go a long way to hold on to those things. Money and love – and self-protection. As much as Maddie liked Catalina, she had to consider her.

And there were the children. Juan-Antonio could be an artist now, free of his father's suffocating expectations. And could something really have been going on between him and Señor Otero's son? Sofia could marry the man she loved. Like Señor Fernandez, Jake Silverstein could have his fair lady, too. But what about Ricardo himself and romance? Sofia didn't think her father had a mistress, but surely he would have kept such a thing hidden. And it seemed as if Diego, the handsome manservant, was making some money somewhere. From blackmail? But who was he blackmailing? What secrets did he know?

And there was money. Ricardo's business, so necessary to maintain his grand house and his position in society, didn't seem to be doing very well, and he'd made lots of people angry over those bad real-estate investments. Not just George Marulis, Sofia's potential fiancé.

Then there were things she hadn't considered before then. She thought of the beautiful Montoya house, the works of art on the wall, and that odd Velázquez Juan-Antonio had created.

What was it about that piece that seemed so 'off'? Could Ricardo have been in some kind of smuggling or forgery deal, beyond that one piece, to make up for those business losses? Or did it come back around to Juan-Antonio? Then again, maybe it was something she couldn't see because she hadn't been in Santa Fe long enough, old family feuds or grudges.

Maddie frowned, and tapped her pencil on the edge of the table as she studied that too-meager collection of information. Then she remembered one more tidbit – those hairs on Ricardo's sleeve. They did look like something familiar. Catalina said they had no pets, as Ricardo didn't like them. Which surely meant he wouldn't have gone near Will's dog Teddy, who had yellowish fur anyway. And Ricardo always seemed so elegant in his dress, tailored suits and fine silk waistcoats, linen shirts.

But maybe . . .

She glanced, startled, at her easel, where her freshly washed brushes waited for her in their jar. She snatched one up, and studied it in the sunlight.

Yes! 'You dang nabbit fool, Maddie,' she murmured. Why had she not seen it before? The hairs on the sleeve were surely the bristles from a paintbrush, a brush made of hog hair, with its interlocked tip. She hadn't seen it at first, as she usually used sable brushes for the soft, fine tip they gave. Not many people she knew often used hog-hair brushes, yet she'd seen them somewhere lately, she was sure of it. Where was it?

She closed her eyes, and tried to remember all the places she'd visited lately. The museum, El Delirio . . .

Of course. It was Paul Vynne's casita at Will's house. They'd been propped on the palette among the clutter of that little space, among other brushes and squeezed-out tubes. But unlike the rest, they'd been clean, as if he hadn't used them recently.

Ricardo must have been near those brushes to get them on his sleeve. But why would he have been in the casita? Paul was a newcomer to Santa Fe, passing through. How would he and Ricardo know each other? Ricardo had been in the East for school as a young man, just as he wanted to send Juan-Antonio there now. Maybe they had once encountered each other there, somehow?

She had to tell Inspector Sadler. Yet how could she make those jagged puzzle pieces fit together, make the picture clear and bright? She couldn't just babble to him about brushes and shoes. He'd always thought her a dumb Dora, as she'd thought him a crasher-througher. They'd just begun to tentatively work together.

She had to find something concrete to give him, something that made it all secure. It had to make sense!

She tossed off her smock and hurried into the house to grab a coat and hat. Surely everyone at Will's would be out today, getting their wagons ready for the Desfile de la Gente, or the Hysterical Parade. She would have a brief time to look around, find that last puzzle piece that could prove her theory was right. As she rushed past the kitchen door, Juanita called, 'We have to try on your costume, Señora Maddie!'

'I just have one quick, tiny errand, Juanita,' she answered. She couldn't tell her, either, until she had the proof. 'I'll get some pastries for the girls at Kaune's on the way back!'

FIFTEEN

It was quiet at Will's as Maddie knocked at the door and peeked in the window. Teddy the dog slept on a hassock, but no one else was around. She had a little time, then, to be a proper snoop. She crossed the garden and hurried up the slope to the casita, making sure no one was around before she eased the door open and slipped inside. It was as messy as she remembered, but surely there was something buried in there that would tell a tale.

First she examined the brushes. Just as she'd remembered, the boar's hair was clean. One of them had a cracked handle, the wood beginning to splinter, and it was tossed aside on the edge of the table. Were there hairs missing? She couldn't quite tell, it was a fine quality brush, tightly bound, though unlike the others it was matted with some paint deep in the hairs. Had Paul or Ricardo grabbed it and broken it in anger?

She glanced across the shadowed room and tried to imagine a fight. It was a small space, and it was such a mess, it looked like struggles took place there regularly anyway! How had it gotten so cluttered in such a short time?

She carefully replaced the brushes where she found them, and examined the shoes tossed in a pile by the door. They were all dusty, but she didn't recognize any of the small pebbles from the arroyo. One pair looked scrubbed clean and freshly cleaned, the brown suede a bit stained along the edge. With blood?

A small desk sat under the back window, and it was tidier than the other tables. She studied a stack of books, poetry, Vasari. There wasn't much in the two drawers, pencils, postcards. She ruffled through the book pages, and found two torn photos and a note tucked inside the back of one of them. *My most darling Paul . . . your arms around me . . . wished the night never ended . . .*

'Don't read that!' she told herself sternly, and felt her cheeks burning as she tucked the note back where she found it. She studied the photos, but they were old and blurry, the torn remains just showing part of figures against a hedgerow, possibly wearing academic robes. Were they like the photos she'd found in Ricardo's desk? The same people? Was that the connection?

She tucked them back where she found them, and made her way outside, and around to the back of the casita. At the dip of the slope, where Will's property led to a narrow path back to another arroyo, she found a ragged firepit, smaller than Zozobra's remains. Reaching for a stick, she poked carefully at the ashes. And struck treasure. Another photo, charred but not completely burned away. She dusted it off and studied the faded faces.

Paul Vynne, young and glowing, his arms around – Ricardo Montoya, also young, his spectacles gleaming in the lost light, kissing Paul's chcck. The scene, frozen and gone so long, pulsed with emotion and joy. Perhaps it was Ricardo who sometimes went to the Golden Rooster.

Hardly able to breathe as time slowed down all around her, she felt like she was swimming in syrup even as she had to hurry-hurry-hurry. She carefully put down the photo and covered it all up again, and backed away. Only when she was at the edge of the slope again did she turn to run.

Surely it was Paul Vynne who killed Ricardo. Paul who once cared for Ricardo. But why? How had it happened? It was hard to imagine that sad-eyed artist in a blazing rage, forcing a man's head underwater and then trying to chop him up. Especially if he had once loved him. Yet she knew all too well that everyone had secrets, some of them dark indeed. Surely there was something she was missing that would make it all suddenly snap together.

Think, think! her brain shouted at her. She stumbled on a rock at the corner of Will's garden and reeled around, her ankle giving a painful twinge. She hobbled on, and suddenly heard Will's voice call her name.

'Are you looking for me, Maddie?' he said, and she whirled around to see that he was not alone. Paul Vynne was with him, the two of them watching her curiously.

She couldn't bring herself to even look at Paul. She summoned up every bit of acting skill she had, honed in her mother's stuffy drawing rooms, and smiled brightly. *Too* brightly? 'Oh! I just had a question about – about the masquerade ball, but I realized the answer myself, so silly. I should get home to start to dress!'

'Paul says you were at the museum and met Herr Rotheim,' Will said.

'Yes, and Juan-Antonio Montoya. Isn't it marvelous that he's going to have art instruction at last?' She realized she was babbling, but she didn't know what to say, what to do. She couldn't stop thinking about the photo she found, of Paul watching her. They talked a bit longer before she managed to excuse herself.

She rushed away, trying to ignore her wretched ankle. She could feel someone watching her go, a tingle at the back of her neck, and knew she couldn't stumble, couldn't give away her thoughts and fears.

Once she finally got back to the top of Canyon Road, she didn't turn toward her house or toward the grocery, but down another lane to cut to the police station. There was no putting it off anymore. She had to tell Sadler what she knew. Sadler wasn't there, though, only the young constable behind the desk.

'I'm sorry, Mrs Alwin,' Rickie said, his eyes widening at her disheveled state. 'The inspector is at Pecos today. Break-ins. Do you – do you want to leave a note, or something?'

She exhaled in frustration. Such slow going, all that trouble, and the man wasn't even there! 'Oh, all right.' She reached for the notebook Rickie offered, and scribbled *It was Paul Vynne in the Montoya case! Meet me at the masquerade ball at La Fonda as soon as you get this.* She could hardly write down every bit of information she'd found at the casita, but that would have to do. Surely it was enough to make Sadler hurry.

Maddie barely remembered she'd promised the twins some

sweets from Kaune's, and she knew she couldn't go home without them. After she stopped at the grocery and turned at last toward home, the ankle was screaming at her. She hobbled through her gate, and glanced across the garden to Gunther's house. It was silent, the windows dark, and her studio was closed up tight. The dogs weren't even barking.

'I'm back, Juanita!' she called as she stepped into the sitting room. It was very quiet in the house, *too* quiet. 'Aren't the girls home from school? I know I'm wretchedly late, but I do have a good excuse.'

Juanita appeared in the kitchen doorway, drying her hands on a towel as she studied Maddie with a quizzical expression. 'Pearl and Ruby are in the garden with the dogs, being noisy again. I'm not sure they deserve sweets!'

Maddie frowned. 'I didn't see them there when I came in, or Pansy and Buttercup. It was all quiet.'

Juanita looked startled. 'It can't be. They've been out there since they got home and changed out of their uniforms. I told them I couldn't have them under my feet while I rolled out the pie crust.'

They ducked back outside in one movement, and Maddie barely felt her ankle as they took in the empty garden.

'It's not like them to run off without asking,' Juanita said tightly.

'Not at all like them. I suppose they might have gone to Gunther's, but I don't think he's home.' They hurried back outside, and heard a faint bark carried on the wind. Yet there were no dogs to be found. Juanita finally found them, locked inside Maddie's studio, and they went into panicked flurries of barks when they flew out the door. The girls weren't with them.

Through the misty haze of rising panic, Maddie glimpsed a white flutter on her studio door. A slip of paper tucked there. She grabbed it, and quickly read the faint, penciled lines.

If you don't want La Llorona to get them, meet me at the masquerade ball at La Fonda on the back stairs. Alone. I have to explain.

SIXTEEN

L a Fonda was crowded with partygoers, the noise deafening, rising up to the skylight dome like a cloud of
color and sound. It was all so filled with merriment, and
it made everything even more nightmarish. Maddie dashed
through the lobby and into the Terraza Room where the
costume ball was to be held, scanning frantically through
the masked faces for Paul or the girls or anyone who could
help. They all looked like strangers, a kaleidoscope of feathers
and satins and gaping, laughing expressions.

Maddie held the ruffled skirts of her flamenco dancer
costume out of the way as she hurried across the lobby. She'd
had to change so no one would think her odd at the party, so
she could find the girls fast. The whole hotel hummed with
that party atmosphere, the world flowing on as hers threatened
to fall apart. The ball was the sort of thing that usually made
her spirits bounce, made her want to whirl and dance, but
certainly not that evening. That evening she just felt trapped
in a hazy nightmare.

She curled her fingers tighter on the crumpled ball of the
note. She *had* to get the girls back, hold them safe in her arms.
She couldn't think about anything else, and she knew she had
to stay calm, stay focused on that all-important goal. This was
not the moment to collapse into terrified tears. She could do
that later.

But why, oh why, she berated herself, hadn't she managed
everything in a more rational way in the first place?

She left behind the more crowded spaces of the lobby,
the knots of people around the registration desk and on the
turquoise-cushioned sofas and leather chairs, and hurried
around its shadowed edges to the tall glass windows of the
portal. The dancing, gliding figures beyond looked ghostly.

She couldn't glimpse Paul; even if everyone wasn't disguised, she was sure she'd know his height, his salt and pepper hair. Nor did she see Inspector Sadler or David, or even Eddie, who would be at work there in the hotel. *Don't tell him yet*, Juanita had said, and headed to the police station as Maddie left for La Fonda. It was up to her now to find Pearl and Ruby.

At the back stairs, the note had said. She turned toward the corridors tucked behind the public rooms, past the elevators where more party guests poured out in a tumble of lace ruffles and beribboned masks. It was much quieter back there, the roar of the party fading.

Would he have the girls there, on the back stairs? Would he tell her what actually happened with Ricardo Montoya, help her make sense of her jumbled thoughts, like a kaleidoscope coming into focus at last? Or would he just get rid of her, too?

Maddie sucked in a deep breath, trying to push down that bubble of panic. She made her way toward the end of the corridor. A noise, a soft rustle, pierced the silence of the corridor, and she whirled around, her heart pounding.

It was a maid, no murdering maniac, making her way toward the landing with a stack of linens. She froze, staring back at Maddie with startled brown eyes.

'Are you all right, miss?' she whispered.

Maddie took another breath. 'Could you do something for me?'

'If I can, miss.'

Surely Juanita had time to get to the police station by then. But how long would it take them to find Inspector Sadler and for him to get to La Fonda? 'Could you see if Inspector Sadler – you know him? Victorian mustache, red face, bowler hat all the time?'

The maid giggled a bit despite the tension. 'I know him.'

'See if he's at the party, and if he is tell him Mrs Alwin needs him most urgently here at those stairs. And tell him for heaven's sake to go quietly for once!'

The maid looked rightfully scared, but she nodded. 'I will. Right now, miss!' She dashed away, leaving Maddie alone again.

She ran toward the stairwell that led up to the rooftop tower. There was surely a party up there now, dancing under the stars as the Fiesta crowds flowed past to the plaza far below, but the stairs were empty. Partygoers would take the elevators. Her shoes clicked, a bit faltering because of her ankle, deafeningly loud to her ears, on the uncarpeted treads. She was sure she could hear her own heart pounding, and she blinked in the dim lights that turned everything murky.

At the landing just below the last flight of steps to the roof, she finally saw him. He looked a bit like La Llorona himself in a long, dark coat, his face ghostly greenish-white in the shadows. He stood very still as he watched her.

'Mr Vynne – Paul,' she said, softly, evenly. She took the last steps very slowly, as if he was a skittish horse who could bolt at any moment, which was just what it looked like now. 'I'm here alone, just as you asked. What is it you have to explain? Are the girls safe?'

He looked startled. 'Certainly they're safe. I wouldn't hurt children. I couldn't hurt anyone!'

Maddie clenched her fist tight before she could shout that he most certainly *had* hurt someone. He'd killed a man! And surely he'd terrified the twins. 'It was an accident, then? Ricardo Montoya?'

'Of course it was. No matter what he did, no matter what he said, he was still my Richard underneath all that. I just wanted to find him again.'

Maddie took one more slow step until she stood on the landing with him. Her breath felt caught in her chest, time sliding into a crawl. 'You knew him before?' she said, thinking of the torn photos.

'When I was a young man. So young and foolish. He was at university when I was in art school, and he was so different from anyone else I'd ever known. So full of life and vigor. Yet so kind, so understanding.'

Maddie swallowed hard at the tenderness in those words. 'You loved him?'

His voice roughened, as if caught on a sob. 'So much. *You* must understand that. You lost someone, too. Your husband.'

Maddie nodded, though she knew very well she would

never have killed Pete if he came back. She had no idea what could drive someone like Paul to do such a thing, but she had to try. To make him think she knew. 'I do understand, yes. You – you probably didn't expect to ever see him again, and when you did it must have felt glorious in that moment. Like no time had ever passed.'

His face brightened with hope. 'Yes, exactly! He was just the same. Outwardly. But inside he was a different person. As if someone else, a monster, had swallowed my Richard. Made him vanish completely.'

'He turned you away?'

'He came to see me that day, the day of Zozobra, when Will had left to fetch supplies. I was so excited to see him at first. Even then, I couldn't believe my Richard could be completely gone! He had to come back to me. I had sent him a note, and he showed me it was in shreds in his pocket.'

'Because he hadn't come back?'

'He told me to – to stay away. He didn't even ask me to leave him to his life, just demanded! If he'd said his life here, his family, was too important to risk and asked me to keep his secret, I would have. I know all about keeping secrets,' he said bitterly. 'I've been doing it my whole life, and I've become good at it. But when I saw your face as you left the casita – I knew I couldn't keep this secret from you. That you had found out.'

'So he was imperious with you? As he was with everyone else?'

Paul gave a harsh laugh that seemed to reverberate all around them in the narrow stairwell. 'He demanded I leave Santa Fe immediately. He offered me money, waved it around in my face with such contempt. Even then I was sure I saw something, a fear in his eyes.'

Maddie thought of what she'd discovered about Ricardo, his deep need for control at all times, and she was sure he must have been afraid. Afraid that control was slipping away forever. She felt a twinge of raw pity despite herself, despite the desperate situation she was in. 'That must have been painful.'

He buried his face in his hands, shaking his head frantically as if it could all be hidden, vanished. 'I've never felt hurt like that. As if I'd been stabbed. I reached for him, so sure if we could only be close again I could tell him – persuade him . . .' He broke off, and looked up with a new coldness in his gaze. 'Will did say you were easy to talk to, that you had a magic sort of understanding.'

'I *want* to understand,' Maddie said, and she realized it was true. Mostly what she wanted was Pearl and Ruby safely back, that was paramount. But even after all Paul Vynne had done, she couldn't help but feel for him. Society expected so much of people, too much; expected them to deny their true selves. 'You loved him, and you lost him. He had even lost himself for all these years.'

'Yes, exactly. I only wanted my Richard back, just for a moment. I thought he was still there somewhere, that he remembered as I did, but that man was never there at all. He hit me when I reached for him. He shoved me away, and I . . .' He broke off again, shaking his head. 'I hit him back, on instinct. I had to! He had me cornered back there where the tub was, that man with my Richard's face who wasn't him at all. I hit him much harder than I thought, and he wasn't expecting it. He lunged for me and lost his balance, his foot caught on a rock and he tripped. The edge of the tub was behind me, and when I dodged away he hit his head on it, with a loud crack. Blood came out of his head, so much blood!'

'And you didn't pull him out of the tub? Out of the water?' Maddie cried.

Paul frantically shook his head. 'I tried! He was so heavy, though, so still. Finally I did haul him out, but there was no pulse. Blood still oozed out of his head, but he was – he was dead. I knew it then. I had killed him. I didn't really know if it was the fight, or if he'd drowned, but I would be blamed. Maybe Will would be blamed, too!'

'So you just – just chopped him up?' Maddie couldn't even fathom such a scene.

'I couldn't be caught. In a strange town, like this. I couldn't let what Richard and I once had become common knowledge. I shouldn't have done it. I'm not that sort of person! How can I be, when I love art so much, when my whole life has been trying to create beauty? I just – couldn't think straight. I'd read about this in a book, you see. A detective novel.'

'You didn't *think*?' she gasped.

That harsh laugh escaped again. 'Clearly not, for I made such a hash of it all. I couldn't even chop properly, could I? I once took anatomy classes, but it was all harder than I thought it could be. I meant to take apart the whole hand, the arm, to hide it all easier. I managed to haul him away to that ditch, but there were – things left behind.'

'The spectacles, and finger,' Maddie said with a shudder, remembering the scene. 'You put them in Zozobra.'

'I didn't know what else to do. People were coming, I didn't have much more time to myself, and I had to clean it all up somehow.'

'Because you hated him so much after all that happened. For his rejection?'

'Because I *loved* him. I've always thought of him, always remembered him, dreamed of him. No one else could match him. But that man didn't exist any longer. When he laughed at me, threatened me . . .' He stopped. 'I lost my way.'

'Where are the girls?' Maddie demanded. 'No matter what happened to you, Paul, you don't want to hurt them, I know you don't. They're innocent of all this. Tell me where they are, please.'

'I told you, I'm not that sort of man! I'm not. I would never hurt them.' A new, frightening level of desperation roughened his voice.

'But you *have* hurt them. They must be so scared. You know what you have to do, to find your own soul again, Paul. Tell me where Pearl and Ruby are, and talk to the police. Tell them the truth.'

'Room 312. But I won't go to the police! And I won't, can't let you do that, either, I'm sorry. So sorry!' He grabbed her arm suddenly, hard, bruising, and she felt herself start to stumble backward, to tumble down the stairs. She instinctively kicked out at him with her heeled shoe, digging it into his ankle until he let her go and fell backward himself.

Maddie screamed, and ran down the stairs on legs shaking so hard she was sure she would collapse. Her ankle was agony, but she ran on as fast as she could, hoping he couldn't get up and chase her. She glimpsed Sadler coming up the stairs toward her, and she would never have imagined she'd be so glad to see that man's ridiculous mustache in all her life. When she babbled to him about what had just happened, he went back up the stairs to kneel down beside Paul.

'He's alive, I think,' she called to him. 'Unconscious, though. Or I couldn't have gotten away.'

'Well, call an ambulance! I thought I saw Dr Cole coming into the hotel, too. Go now!' Sadler barked. He glanced down at Maddie, his expression filled with some admiration and a lot of anger. 'So this is the killer, is it?'

Maddie swallowed hard, and nodded. 'It – it was an accident. He didn't mean to kill Montoya.'

'He tried to chop up a body on accident?' Sadler scoffed.

'Yes, he – oh, I'll tell you everything later, Inspector! I have to find the girls.' She whirled around and rushed down the stairs to the next floor, not slowing down at all until she reached #312. She burst inside, hardly daring to breathe – and saw Pearl and Ruby perched on the bed with a pile of movie mags and a big box of Milk Duds.

'Miss Maddie!' Pearl said happily. 'Did you read that *Thief of Baghdad* cost over a million dollars to make! Is there that much money in the world?'

'Shocking stuff,' Ruby agreed.

Maddie burst into tears, and grabbed the girls up for the tightest hug ever.

SEVENTEEN

The party in Maddie's house was in full swing, every window filled with light, music seeping out. Juanita and Father Malone moved toward the dining room, carrying trays of more biscochitos and Juanita's extra-special rarely made chocolate cherry cake. Gunther poured champagne, and the girls bounced around with the dogs, delighted to get to stay up late and seemingly suffering no after-effects of their kidnapping.

Maddie leaned back on her garden chaise and stared up at the starry sky. So endless, all those stars swirling like sequins scattered on purple velvet. All had ended well – for her. She had her home and family safe and secure again, but that sadness, that fear, lingered. She shivered and closed her eyes, and heard a footstep on the garden path, smelled that hint of lemony soap, and knew it was David. She smiled, and held out her hand to him.

'I thought you might be cold out here.' He wrapped a cashmere shawl around her, and sat down beside her to hold her close. She snuggled even closer, burying her face in his shoulder to inhale his delicious scent, like the air after rain.

'Are you sure you're well, Maddie darling?' he said. 'I could give you another powder . . .'

'I'm absolutely the bee's knees, David, really, since the girls are home safe,' she said. 'I just – well, I suppose I do feel sorry for Paul, despite everything. He'd held the pain of that love inside for so very long.'

'That's understandable. It's a sad situation. For everyone.'

'What do you think will happen to him once he's out of the hospital?'

'Physically, he will be well. A concussion from the fall, soon mended. Legally – I don't know. You could fit my knowledge of the law into an eggcup. I do think perhaps mitigating circumstances.'

'Would Sadler see it that way?'

David laughed, and kissed the top of her head. 'It seems like our inspector is softening a bit. He just had a third helping of Juanita's casserole in there, and asked how it was made. Very strange. Maybe he'll have some compassion.'

If even the inspector could change, surely there was hope for anyone. 'Still, I can't help but feel sorry for them all,' she whispered.

David leaned his cheek against her hair, his arms safe around her, holding her above any cold or fear. 'Sorry for Montoya or Paul Vynne?'

'Both, I suppose. I know it was a terribly gruesome thing to happen. But to feel that much for so long . . .' She glanced toward her lovely house, where everything was just as she wanted it to be, where she could see her friends through the brightly lit windows. Where she had built her own world.

She'd built up a safe haven. Not everything could be kept out, yet so many good things were brought in. She could always be herself there, and know she was loved anyway. 'I'm so, so lucky, David. I was able to make my own life, my own world. I only wish I could build it that way for everyone.'

He drew her even closer. 'I came a very long way looking for – well, I didn't know *what* I was looking for, not then. I was just running away from things, really. But I knew very well I needed a new start,' he said.

Maddie nodded against his shoulder. 'I did the same. I always felt so restless in my life, ever since I was a little girl. After Pete, I knew there was nothing left for me in New York, not if I really wanted to find out who I was. Who I *am*.'

'And you've found it here?'

'Yes. My house, my sky, my real family.' And this man. Especially this man, with his strength and kindness and intelligence, his acceptance. And his handsome blue eyes.

'So have I, Maddie. I found what I didn't even know I missed so much.'

She looked up at him in the moonlight. He looked back,

intense, intimate. She loved him so very much she was sure she would burst with it. 'Have you, David?'

'I found love here. That's the most important thing of all, isn't it?'

'L–love?' she whispered. They had never said those words before. She hadn't realized how much she really longed for them.

'I love you, Madeline Vaughn-Alwin. I think I have ever since I first saw you on that train. I'd never seen anyone so beautiful before.'

'I love you, too. So, so much!' she cried.

'So,' he said. 'Should we get married? Someone has to be with you when you go running after murderers.'

Maddie laughed at those words. *Should we get married.* The simple abruptness of them, the perfection. 'I'm not really planning to chase a murderer again, but if I must there is no one I would rather have with me than you, David Cole. So yes. I definitely think we should get married. *Definitely.* Yes.'

EPILOGUE

It was truly a glorious wedding. The cathedral was awash in golden, red, blue, green light from the stained-glass windows, sunshine streaming over the altar like a river of liquid gilt. Everywhere a person turned, there were white satin streamers, towering arrangements of lilies and roses scenting the air with their summery perfume. Feathered hats nodded along to the music from the organ, and flower girls scattered their petals over the blue aisle carpet with great abandon and panache. It was all that Maddie, and especially the twins with their awestruck gazes under their new hair bows, could have dreamed.

And Sofia Montoya was absolutely radiant as she glided up the aisle on her brother's arm between the sage green and gold pillars, through the crowds massed on the polished pews. She looked like a cloud of tulle, silk, and lace, her mother's mantilla draped over her hair. Catalina wept and laughed alternately, holding André Fernandez's hand when 'The king of love my shepherd is' rolled through the soaring space. Father Malone, in his white and gold vestments, beamed.

And Jake Silverstein's eyes shimmered as he watched his bride come toward him. It seemed to take all his best man's powers to hold him back from dashing to meet her. Even though it was said they had already been married by a rabbi, and Jake should be used to bridal matters now.

It was a perfect day all around. And not a single murder to mar it.

Maddie took it all in, finding it hard to believe everything ended so well after all. Juanita and the twins sniffled into their handkerchiefs on one side of her, and Maddie was sure she would cry a bit herself before too long. She thought of her own wedding, so long ago now. A quick, hurried ceremony in the rectory of Grace Church before Pete went off to war, but sweet and loving and perfect in its own way.

As Sofia and Jake clasped hands, beaming at each other, Maddie *did* sniffle a bit behind the short, fluttering net veil of her new sky-blue cloche hat. David, sitting beside her, slid her a handkerchief.

'Thank you, darling. You are always quite prepared,' she whispered, and tried to blow her nose in a dainty way. 'Isn't it all a bit – wistful? Weddings and such.'

He gave her a puzzled smile, and squeezed her hand. 'Wistful? I rather enjoy weddings, myself. There's always cake afterwards.'

'And sometimes champagne.' She looped her arm through his, and watched as Sofia and Jake knelt together, the very image of *romance*, both so young and gorgeous and glowing with the sheer force of their happiness. Catalina and André looked happy, too, smiling up at each other. And Juan-Antonio would soon be off on his art studies. Something terrible had ended in something so – right.

Maddie glanced up at David, his bright silver-and-gold hair like a halo from the stained-glass light.

'Do you think our wedding will be just like this?' she whispered, and for an instant she pictured more roses, more satin, more music.

He smiled, and she shivered with the beauty of it. She forgot every image of lace and cake, and just saw *him*. 'Oh, Maddie. It will be so much better. In fact, it will probably be the very best wedding ever.'

She laughed in delight, sure she would float away into the arched rafters. 'Yes. If no one gets murdered, that is . . .'

AUTHOR'S NOTE

I'm so excited to be back in Maddie's world of 1920s Santa Fe! Though I live here, and so much of what she loved in this place is still what I love (the weather, the art, the food!), there's a lot that has changed, too. And that's true of Fiesta, a week of remembrance and celebration that has changed and evolved over the years, but which is still here. (My dogs love the Desfile de los Ninos, or Pet Parade as its also known, where children and their dogs/cats/guinea pigs/ whatever they have, put on a colorful and joyous parade!)

Fiesta has its origins in 1692, when the Spanish who were driven out by the Pueblo Revolt twelve years before, returned, led by Don Diego de Vargas. In 1712, the Spanish governor of the province proclaimed a religious commemoration of those events, where there were Masses, processions, and family dinners. This didn't change for many years, but had much lapsed by the 1760s.

In 1912, the Chamber of Commerce thought Fiesta ready for a revival – as a commercial scheme. They organized events that often didn't have much to do with New Mexico, and charged entry fees which shut out many locals and it was meant to draw more tourists to the new state. In the 1920s, a group of artists, led by Will Shuster, protested this and organized their own "El Pasatiempo". complete with many of the events we have now – parades, dances, and especially Zozobra! (There are still traditional events, as well, such as Novenas and Masses, and the procession of La Conquistadora, a wooden figure of The Virgin Mary brought to Santa Fe in 1692 and now housed in the Cathedral.)

Will Shuster was one of the great characters of Santa Fe in the twentieth century! Born in Pennsylvania in 1893, he came to New Mexico with his wife in 1920 for his health (he was gassed in World War I) and to pursue his dreams of being an artist. His natural gregariousness and creativity made him a leader, especially among a group who lived near him called Los Cinco Pintores (or "five little nuts in five mud huts", as some wags called them!). He was constantly throwing parties, organizing events, getting into scrapes. One of his most enduring parties is Zozobra, or "Old Man Gloom". Made of wool, wire, and cotton cloth, he now reaches 50 feet high and his burning is attended by around 70,000 people, who crowd into a park to contribute their "glooms" (anxieties or bad events, written on slips of paper to be packed in and around the giant marionette). In 1924, Zozobra was only about 6 feet high, a puppet in Shuster's garden to amuse his artist friends. As far as I know, there were no body parts found in the ashes that year! By 1926, he realized it was a popular thing and moved to a park for others to see. On Shuster's death in 1969, he left the rights to the Zozobras party to the Kiwanis Club, and it is run every year as a charitable fundraiser (and gloom-burner).

The White sisters, Elizabeth and Martha, were also real figures in 1920s Santa Fe! The college-educated daughters of a wealthy Pennsylvania newspaper magnate, they were on a cross-country trip to California after the War (where Elizabeth served as a nurse), and decided to stay in Santa Fe, where they built their large compound "El Delirio" (named after their favorite bar in Seville, Spain!). Elizabeth lived a long, energetic life as a patron of the arts, breeder of Irish wolfhounds (she liked to march them in the Fiesta parades!), and Native American rights activist. Their home is now the School of Advanced Research, and has a wonderful library where I've done much research! They were the first home in town to have a tennis court and swimming pool, and the party to inaugurate the pool was a real event! (Complete with poem by Witter Bynner, another of the great characters of Santa Fe!)

A few sources I've found very helpful are:
– Joseph Dispenza and Louise Turner, Will Shuster: A Santa Fe Legend (1989)
– Edna Robertson, Los Cinco Pintores (1975)

– Jennifer Owings Dewey, Zozobra: The Story of Old Man Gloom
   – Gregor Stark and E. Catherine Rayne, El Delirio: The Santa Fe World of Elizabeth White (1998)
   – Stacia Lewandowski, Light, Landscape, and the Creative Quest: Early Artists of Santa Fe (2011)
   – Van Deren Coke, Taos and Santa Fe: The Artists' Environment 1882-1942 (1963)
   – Edna Robertson, Artists of the Canyons and Caminos (2006, reprint)